HOUDINI
HEART

Books by Ki Longfellow

China Blues*
Chasing Women*
Stinkfoot, a Comic Opera (with Vivian Stanshall)
The Secret Magdalene
Flow Down Like Silver: Hypatia of Alexandria

*Early editions as Pamela Longfellow

KI LONGFELLOW'S

HOUDINI HEART

Eio Books

Published in the United States by

Eio Books
1550 Tiburon Boulevard
Suite B-9
Belvedere, California, 94920 U.S.A.

www.eiobooks.com

Library of Congress Cataloging-in-Publication Data

Longfellow, Ki
  Houdini Heart / Ki Longfellow
    p. cm.
ISBN 978-0-9759255-1-5 (alk. paper)
1. Women authors --Fiction. 2. Vermont --Fiction. 3. I. Title.
  PS3562.O499 H68 2011
  813'.54

                              2011012001

Cover designed by Shane Roberts
Book designed by Shane Roberts
Cover image: River House
Cover photo by Shane Roberts

10 9 8 7 6 5 4 3 2 1

First Paperback Edition

For Silky

Perhaps larks and katydids dream. Perhaps absolute reality, as Shirley Jackson once wrote, is absolutely insane.

Given a moment of thought, what the hell is *absolute* reality? Reality, pure or impure, certain or uncertain, is an illusion. So too is insanity. Perhaps death is the ultimate illusion. Perhaps I am already dead.

Of course larks and katydids dream. We all of us dream. What else is reality but dreaming?

River House was a palace when I was nine. When I was nine I intoxicated myself by calling it haunted. A haunted palace. Behind its thick brick walls and tall-windowed rooms, I imagined people laughing, people dancing, people saying things that mattered...and behind them—another world of lunatic darkness they could not see.

From the sidewalk across the Main Street of Little Sokoki, Vermont, my unlettered, foul-mouthed, dishonest mother dragging me along by the arm, I would look back at it, dreaming, for as long as I could.

1

Almost twelve when we had to skip town,
the last time I saw River House I was crammed
in with a stray kitten I'd begged to keep, and all
my mother's other junk in the back of her aging
Plymouth station wagon.

By then, River House was only a hotel. Just
another hotel.

For the past few years, I've been thirty-six years
old. The years flicker by, and with them my mostly
unremembered life, yet I'm not getting wiser. Or
deeper. Slyer, perhaps. Of necessity, much slyer.
I've begun to think I might be slow. Or maybe
empty. I'd even settle for "repressed" if that meant
I was damaged goods, another casualty of early
neglect or abuse.

But the truth is, I suspect I'm no more than
my mother was: clever, but not all that bright. No
real depth, what the Brits call "bottom." This is
probably why I'm not the writer I hoped I would be.

What the hell. Like my mother, I'm also a liar.
Because my mother lied, I have no idea who I am,
where I came from. Because I lie, neither does
anyone else.

I am thirty-six and I'm home again. Or at least
back in Little Sokoki. I had to come somewhere. I
had to stop somewhere. And Little Sokoki fills a
primary need: they won't think to look for me here.
At least not right away.

Stepping out of a Vermont Trailways bus all
these years later, weighted down with a large
leather shoulder bag and my laptop, I'm in the town
we stayed in the longest—even now, three years
seems a very long time. Of all the places I lived
with my rootless feckless hopeless mother, Little

Sokoki, Vermont, was my favorite. Because of the river. Because of River House.

Of course now that I'm here, I can see that I've changed—I've changed a great deal. In this town, I used to stand awestruck by tiny purple flowers hidden in the grass, by the shape of roots in the deep woods, by the curve of sweet water lured by the salt sea, by my own elfin shadow on walls. Now they mean nothing. I barely notice them. I'd like to think it's a loss of innocence, but really I've been spoiled, as in "corrupted." I've come to know what a palace looks like. A palace looks like certain great houses in Paris, London, New York, Vienna, Barcelona, Beverly Hills. Like certain hotel rooms I could afford for awhile. When my star was on the rise. When I was the *l'artiste de l'heure* and had won a prestigious literary prize. When the prize had turned into speaking tours, the book turned into a movie—and the prize and the movie turned my head. When I would say things like *l'artiste de l'heure.*

Thinking back, and even with the excuse of youth, I sicken myself.

I'm not surprised to find River House has not become yet again a palace. For one thing, it's too small. Nor is it glamorous or fey. It's still a handsome building; as handsome and as ordinary as many of the old buildings still upright in New England. Stores diminish its ground floor: a Rexall, an Italian restaurant, an opticians, a shop selling lingerie, a dark dusty space with a large "For Rent" sign in its window, a half decent bookstore. (I've already looked. I am not in it.) Worse, its small theater, once a home for roving players, is now become a small movie house showing one of

3

Joel's efforts. Disturbing to see the thing here.
Disturbing to think my recent neighbor from across
a winding Malibu road's big budget movie got to
Little Sokoki before I did.

Not a palace, River House is also no longer
a hotel. Above its shops and movie house, it's
an apartment building. Its ceilings lowered, its
wide airy rooms chopped into kitchenettes and
"efficiency units," its flaws painted and painted
again, the revolving door torn out long ago, my
wonderful "haunted" hotel is gone.

But then, so am I.

I have fled to the town of my youth, and alone.
If I am careful, I have money enough to last me six
months, maybe seven. In these last months, I will
finally live in River House, rent one of its cheapest
studio "units," eat very little, buy less, maybe see a
movie or two. I will write one more book and in it I
will give all that I have left to give, and then, if it's
the usual crap—I'll kill myself.

Assuming it'll be crap, this is my suicide note.

(Note to self: Walker Percy said, "...suicide
seems to help sell books." I'd add: but it doesn't
guarantee talent.)

There. I've made a beginning. Perhaps I have
half a year to live. Perhaps not. Standing on Main
Street, looking up at what's happened to River
House, I see it doesn't matter.

My third floor room in River House is shabby.
Lying on my bed, a futon hastily purchased when
I found the room unfurnished, I'm staring up at
the ceiling. Once an elegant height, now it is eight

feet from the floor, a useful American distance—
the height of a sheet of plywood. To lower it,
whoever "remodeled" my once entrancing hotel has
crisscrossed the gracious old ceiling with cheap
aluminum supports and on these, placed thin
plastic ceiling tiles. They're meant to come away
easily in case of fire. And they do. They come away
so easily, every time I open or close my door one or
another of them falls out of the ceiling. I've given
up putting them back. Now they're in a stack in
one of my empty corners. The tiles were meant to
be cream colored. It's hard to tell under the deep
yellow stain of age and nicotine. We who live here
are not allowed to smoke in our rooms. Judging by
the ceiling tiles, I must be the only one who obeys.
There is one wall in each apartment made of rough
wood. The management calls this wall a "feature."
I suspect someone found an old barn and bought
its wood on the cheap. All the kitchens have thirty-
year-old "harvest gold" refrigerators and "harvest
gold" stoves. The gold is a thin mustardy yellow.
Very ugly. The small cabinets over the metal sinks
are dark brown and sticky with ancient cooking oil.
Very ugly. The cheap carpets are industrial brown.
Unspeakably ugly.

If River House weeps, who could blame it?

But they couldn't ruin the windows. The
windows are still tall and still filled with the thick
wavy glass of years and years ago.

Looking through them, the town below could
be beneath the sea. Or under the river. Its streets
and buildings and sidewalks are curved. Or bent.
Or, in some places, missing.

CHAPTER ONE

This is as far as I've gotten. Two words staring back at me from my computer screen. I begin with no plans for this last novel, no treatment or outline. I haven't even a theme (not that I have ever had a theme), and I certainly don't know my story. But I've decided to rely on trust. It will come. It will tell itself to me if I just sit here long enough, stay awake, stop day-dreaming.

I shall take a walk. Down to the river that runs along the eastern flank of Vermont. Before I go out, I make sure that my door is locked. Half way to the elevator, I worry: what if I haven't really locked it? I tell myself I've locked the door. I am safe. But what if I'm not? I walk back to check it. It's locked. Now I tell myself not to lose my keys.

Somewhere over the years I've been gone, Little Sokoki seems to have begun thinking of itself as a city. It acts like a city. There are a few city people here come up from Massachusetts to inflict their city ways on it. I turn away. I've seen enough of their anger and despair in other places, heard enough of their brutal talk, their brutal music. They do not dream: they demand. They do not imagine: they watch and they envy. They do not read. To them, the few words they know are weapons. Who are they to me and me to them? Although they *do* go to the movies. Which is why so many movies have become what they are: brutal, stupid, and crude. (Like the perfect example my brutal, stupid, crude, very successful and very rich neighbor produced, now playing at the River House Movie Theater.)

The river is the Connecticut and it is more beautiful in this place than any river I have ever seen. I'm not yet sure, but I think if I have to die by my own hand, I will die in its waters.

Walking along the riverbank in the summer heat, I've come across a fish out of water, dead, dried out, its tail frayed and stiff. There are ants in its eye sockets. There are flies crawling on its pried up scales. There is a bee in its mouth. Staring at it, I realize that if I chose drowning, I will have to find a way to avoid being washed up, become something hideous by the edge of the river. Like Virginia Wolfe throwing herself in the River Ouse at the bottom of her garden, I might put stones in my pockets to weigh myself down, very big stones. I don't think I will be able to bear busy ants carrying me away, very tiny piece by very tiny piece, where someone could come by and watch them.

Back in my room again.

Filed away on my laptop, there is a copy of each of my five books. This is how *The Windigo's Daughter* began, the one that won me my prize, the one that was filmed with a surprising cast of fairies. I'll put that another way. Its cast played surprising fairies. I'll try that again. The cast, playing fairies of one sort or another, surprised me with their willingness to play fey outside something written by Shakespeare. They also played horror because *The Windigo's Daughter* was a horror story. Just like this one.

*Many years ago (or now if you prefer),
there was once a wild and wonderful land,
full of wild and wonderful people—but more
wonderful still, were its creatures.*

*It wasn't yet called Vermont, but it would
be.*

*At that time, magic walked the earth by
day and by night, and the very air shivered
with an ancient pizzazz.*

*Most magical of all was Catamount, slick
as soap, gaudy as a neon sign. There was
Shagamaw Bear, tall as a cedar and fierce as
a thistle. And Azeban, the Raccoon, tricky as
a cardsharp. Moose stood, placid as an oboe,
subtle as a tuba. While Beaver held classes
in architecture. And Elephant had hair down
to his knees. There was Turkey, bone in her
throat. And Otkon, skinned in aniline blue,
bathing in bog mud and hissing like a high
tension wire. Firefly was a pencil of light
writing poems on the dusk. And Turtle, who
lived in a house of cucumber green, mumbled
wisdom all the day long.*

*And then there were the little people, the
Manogemassak, giggling on the riverbanks,
their faces like ax blades, their hearts like
water.*

*While not last and never least, drooled
Windigo, whose hairy knuckles scraped the
forest floor as he ran and whose voice was
like the moaning of the wind.*

*Over all these stood Manitou, cunning as
Houdini, who breathed magic as easily as
breathing air.*

In those days, the weather was always

certain. In winter, the land was thigh-deep in blue snow; in spring, mud. Summer was long and hot and liquid green. Fall was the glory of Manitou.

No doubt, it was always this way, and will remain this way for time everlasting...and then some—but for the Windigo's daughter. Who wasn't bad looking as Windigos go (which is never far enough), but was as restless as the wind over grasses, as willful as the roots of the willow tree. The Windigo's youngest daughter could change things forever, and never look back.

But for now (in your time, in these times), Vermont is a place of green and rolling dairy farms, of covered bridges and boxy Grange Halls, of sugar houses and slender churches, pure white and steepled, of September fairs and ice fishing in February, of small towns easy with assumptions and useful with beliefs. In short, you see a pleasant place, peaceful, perhaps a little romantic.

And of all the small towns in pleasant and peaceful Vermont, Wobanaki Falls is by far the prettiest. And if not the most remote—it's remote enough, lying where the Wobanaki River, rushing cold and clean out of the Green Mountains, flows into the deep blue Connecticut.

It's right here in the town of Wobanaki Falls in the County of Sokoki, Vermont, that our story begins—and ends.

On West Hackmatack Street.

Where Faye, hard as the passing of time but handsome as a Morgan mare, has just

11

come out of her house and is now sitting
on her back porch choosing pebbles for her
slingshot. On the lawn behind her stands an
open tent; under the striped canvas a long
table with a pink cloth. All morning long she's
been trying things on, taking them off, trying
on something else—it's impossible. No matter
how she works it, her slingshot shows under
her wedding gown. Or gets tangled in the
lace.
　　Faye's getting married an hour from now.
　　From farther along West Hackmatack
Street comes the sound of a lawn mower.
Faye stretches her nostrils to catch the scent.
Who's mowing their lawn on her wedding
day?

When I wrote that, I thought I was someone else. Someone who laughed and danced. Someone with thoughts that mattered. Someone who could see in the dark. Someone I will never think I am again. But even then I wrote about Vermont. Even then I thought Vermont was enchanted, that it was full of magic—and palaces. Wobanaki Falls was the name I gave the small town of my childhood. I see I've always been trying to come home.

CHAPTER ONE

Oh, for god's sake. The old woman is walking by my door again.

In the corridors at all hours of the day or night, or riding the elevators, up and down, she must live in River House. I haven't seen her enter or leave

any of the "units," but whichever is hers, she can't
or won't stay in it. Maybe she's afraid of her feature
wall. Or having the tiles of her filthy yellow ceiling
fall on her all at once. If she's waiting for the
elevator and someone else shows up, she pretends
she's forgotten something, steps back, allows it
to go up or down without her. She never speaks
and no one speaks to her. Aside from me, no one
even looks at her. I imagine that's because she's
ugly. Real ugliness is disturbing. If you looked,
you couldn't stop looking. Best not to look at all.
Plus, there's something wrong with her skin besides
age and the fact that she hasn't washed since the
invention of water.

If the old woman is not bad enough, only New
York City makes more noise than Little Sokoki. On
the Rue de Bac, on Hampstead High Street, near
the Ramblas, even on Sunset, the streets seemed
quieter than they are here. It's one in the morning
and they still shout down below in the parking
lot. There is a bar in the basement of River House.
The Last Ditch stretches far under the sidewalk,
maybe even under the street. On Fridays and
Saturdays, it hosts live bands. On Thursdays, it's
open mike night. *The Last Ditch* is very popular. It
means I can't even try to sleep until gone two in the
morning.

Four days of this, and I've already decided to
sleep during the day and to write at night.

I work in bed. Now that I'm here, I do almost
everything in bed. A futon, a lamp, a closet, a
bathroom, a refrigerator to chill the wine I drink,
what else do I need? I do not need company. All
that is done with, finished. Like the stains and the
scuffs and the marks of long gone tenants on my

walls, there's nothing left of my past but the cash we kept for emergencies in a book on our bedroom shelf in the Malibu house. One of his jokes, the book was a hollowed out copy of *Movie Money: Understanding Hollywood's (Creative) Accounting Practices*. 2nd Edition.

All that I loved has turned into money. Even that is almost gone.

CHAPTER ONE

I'm down to a third of a bottle of Riesling, and there she is, walking by my door again. Is she stopping? The footsteps were there, and then they weren't there. I'm listening with half an ear. The other half listens to the glimmer of a story, something I might write about. It's a small idea, not yet worthy of a book, not even of a movie; but it's the first idea I've had in a long time.

There is the smallest scraping outside my door. Timid. Hesitant. If I didn't know about the rancid old woman who wanders the halls of River House (reminds me of a movie, which movie? won't come), and considering the mood I'm in, I might think those sounds something a spider would make. A big spider.

Nothing for it. If I don't answer the door, something tells me she'll stay there, fussing, making her spider sounds. Maybe she needs help. Maybe someone else needs help. A minute of talking to me, she'll see I'm no help to anyone, and then maybe she'll bugger off. I set aside my laptop (on which nothing but CHAPTER ONE is written) and go to my door.

When I open it, no one is there.

It's early afternoon when I awaken. With no shades, no curtains, no Venetian blinds, sunlight falls across my bed like a drunk. If there's one thing I know about, it's falling drunks.

Hot, headachy, shaky, slightly dizzy, I'll shower, then take my notebook, sit in the library for awhile. In the midst of all those books, all those words written by all those other writers, surely there's an idea going begging. The one I had in the middle of the night looks brassy by daylight.

I'm hungry. But it will pass. I can't eat. Food makes me sick. Like a squirrel or a rat, or a Margaret Atwood heroine, I'm learning to live on seeds. Bread and butter sometimes. A piece of fruit. But mostly seeds. And wine.

I'm just about to cross High Street on my way up Main to the Little Sokoki library; I'm waiting for the light to turn green, when, on a whim, I look back at River House. It's what I used to do—stand for as long as I could down on the street, my mother's bony impatient hand attached to my bony stubborn wrist, and gaze up at the five floors of red brick, the roof of rich purple tiles, the whimsical towers at each end of the building (but best is the tallest widest tower on the corner of River House rising above me), at all the tall windows running a third the length of Main, and half the length of High—and I do it now. There's someone in my room. I see someone or something pass across my window, the one innocent of covering on the third floor, and sited under the tallest tower at the angled corner of High Street and Main.

I bolt back through the large outer doors and

15

into the lobby, ignore the elevator which is at the top of the building anyway, and run up the enclosed stairs. If someone is in my room, they're looking at my things. I have nothing to steal, but I have everything to hide.

I locked my door. I know I did. I have my keys in my hand. Did I forget to lock my door? Damn it. Damn it.

My hand is shaking as I try my doorknob. It's locked. I was sure I'd locked it, and I was right—I did lock it. So I unlock it, push open my door. No one is there. Nothing is changed. I walk to the window, look through the wavy glass down onto the sidewalk where I stood looking up only minutes ago. I half expect to see myself there. (Hello, me!)

If someone has been in my room, they are not here now. There is only the one room, an open closet, and the bathroom. My bed is still mussed, the bottom half of my men's pajamas (his pajamas) still hangs from the bathroom knob, my empty glass is on the floor by my pillow, the empty bottle next to it. No one has been here.

I did not mistake what I saw in the window. So. What else? I must have mistaken the window.

Mine is apartment 3-6. It's the smallest of all the units in River House, fitted into the corner of the building. Having seen the floor plan posted on the wall near the manager's office, I've discovered my room is not a square or a rectangle, but a chevron. High Street does not meet Main at an exact right angle. This means that the left wing of River House does not meet the right wing of River House at an exact right angle.

Above or below, there is no other room quite like my room. How could I have mistaken the window?

16

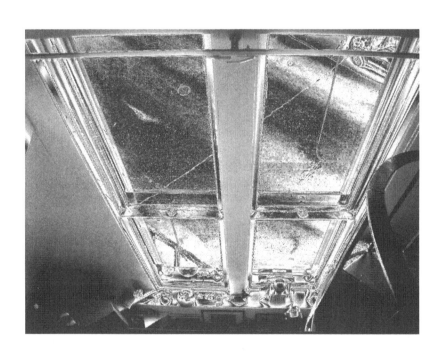

I make it to the library by three. As I did in the book store on the ground floor of River House, I look for my books. By pretending to search for an author whose last name begins with the same letter as mine, I see two of them. *The Windigo's Daughter* and *The White Bee*. For one long moment, I come almost alive. It's not very good (call me surprised), but writing *The White Bee* gave me pleasure.

Pleasure. I've forgotten it. Like awe or excited anticipation or love, I can hardly remember the feeling.

At six o'clock I do not bring back an idea—instead I bring back books. Until I find myself writing, I will read. I've chosen tales of horror and ghost stories. Horror, laced with fairy, worked for me once. Perhaps it will work again. In truth, I chose horror because all I know has come down to that one word—wait. I lie. All that I know has come down to *two* words. Horror. And. Disappointment.

Nothing is as it was. It never was as I hoped it would be. Nothing is.

It's one-thirty in the morning and she's out there again, walking up and down the third floor corridor. This time there is no scraping, no spidery scratching. Only the sound of thick shoes on the thin carpet, slowly approaching and slowly receding, slowly approaching.

This time I will ignore her. I have a book to write.

CHAPTER ONE

I awake to darkness. My light is off. I don't
remember turning it off. My machine is still open
on the bed. Like me, it's been asleep. I lie here for
a moment, getting my bearings, feeling my way. I
am not yet used to being here, not used to having
no proper bed so that essentially I sleep on the
floor. There is no table. There are no chairs. I am
not used to where the window is, the closet, the
bathroom. There is no moon outside, and only the
sound of the occasional car driving in the night.

I get up, move around, replenish my glass.

He used to say we were stuck with each other.
He said that no amount of turning or twisting could
unglue us. And god knows, we both tried. Even
after Kate died, we could not pry loose one from
the other. Most of the time, I cannot remember
his face. But now, perched on a low-slung window
sill in River House, looking down on Main Street at
night, gas lit and finally quiet, I see him clearly. I
see him as he was the last time I really looked at
him: long arms and long legs, toneless white flesh
and thinning yellow hair. Manitou eyed.

He said I had his heart. He'd given me it
the moment we met. Hearing this, I thought of
something Dante wrote.

> *When Love appeared to me so suddenly*
> *That I still shudder at the memory*
> *Joyous Love seemed to me, the while he held*
> *My heart within his hands, and in his arms*
> *My lady lay asleep wrapped in a veil.*
> *He woke her then and trembling and*
> *obedient*
> *She ate that burning heart out of his hand.*

There is a health food co-op here in Little
Sokoki. It's very successful and very expensive.
Healthy wealthy people go there. Or I imagine
they do. I imagine they are healthy and hale
and concerned with the poisons we are fed in the
name of profit. I am already full of poison. What
difference could it make to add more?

In the early afternoon of my eighth day, I've
made my way down Main Street to the Little
Sokoki art deco department store, crossed the
iron footbridge over the Blackstone Brook, passed
the health food co-op, and then walked a further
mile on my own two feet to Price Chopper. Price
Chopper has cheaper wine. Its nuts and seeds
are bagged and salted and no doubt full of toxins.
Waiting in the express line, I can't help looking
through the supermarket tabloids. After all, he's on
the cover of every one of them. And so am I. But
the way I look now, the clothes I wear, who would
know it was me? The woman behind me leans
forward to cluck her tongue. I think she's going to
make some remark about him, some expression of
pity or disgust. Instead she says, "I worry about
Jeannie now that Brent's left her flat for that crazy
Amelie. Jeannie didn't deserve it. You can see
from the photos she's a good girl."

I look at the photos again. I don't see a good
girl. I don't see a bad girl. I see a rich ambitious
woman who's made her choice. I understand
Brent's ex down to the bone. Little kids mess with
ambition, they screw with your art. Little kids are
worse than men. You can't kill your children. My
heart, numb for weeks, begins to bleed. Oh, my
poor little Kate, my poor little Kate. I hide my eyes
so that I might hide my tears. No crying in Price

Chopper. No crying. No bleeding.

Walking the same distance back, someone speaks to me. I am so surprised I come very close to dropping my four bottles of zinfandel. It happens between the River House Theater lobby on the ground floor of River House and the shop for rent.

"Hello," says a voice to my left as I am shifting my plastic bag of wine and seeds from one hand to the other.

It's a young man. He's sitting on a sidewalk bench provided by "The friends of Margaret O'Dell."

I look at him, just long enough to be considered polite, but not long enough to be thought interested. There's an open satchel on the bench by his side. In his hand, he's holding a small camcorder.

"Hello." Even to my own ears, my voice sounds odd. It should sound odd. I have said virtually nothing aloud for more than a month now. No more than I must to make my needs understood. My scratchy unused voice does not stop him. But I am used to that. It happens. If I do not talk, people must judge me by looks alone. By looks alone, I am an attractive woman. But only by looks alone. By looks alone, he is an attractive young man. Exotic, even beautiful. But young. At least ten years younger than I am. Maybe fifteen years younger. Hell, he could be twenty years younger. Not that it matters. He could be exactly my age and it would not matter. I have no interest in young men. Or old men. I have no interest in men at all. Or in children. All of that has been seared away.

He continues to speak. His voice is terrifying. "I've seen you before." I sicken with fear. Here it comes. He knows me. He knows who I am, or

21

who he thinks I am. He knows more than I do. He continues. "Near the elevator." I would begin to relax, but the young man is raising his camcorder. He's aiming it at me. For the first time I notice there is a dog on the bench beside him. The dog is not beautiful. He looks ragged, ill used. One eye is blue, the other red.

I shy violently, making the bottles in my plastic bag clank together. "Don't do that!"

In my room a few moments later, it takes me half an hour to stop shaking.

I forget names as soon as I hear them. I forget faces if they are not constantly in my face. I forget dates and interesting facts and things I've found important only a week before. I forget whether something actually happened to me, or if I only dreamed it. I forget so many things I am surprised to find I have a memory at all. If other people are like me, I am forgotten. If I am forgotten, I am safe.

But other people aren't like me. A killer is rare. Much rarer than books and movies and TV would have you believe.

Leaves of old gold and wine lie scattered on the sidewalks from Cherry Street on the south to Hackmatack Common on the north, pumpkins grin on stoops, white paper ghosts flutter behind windows, and everywhere West Hackmatack goes there are tidy houses set back on tidy lawns.

Faye's house is a small brown saltbox on a small wooded lot snug between Mr. Hunnicutt's white colonial and Mrs. Wheelock's big red brick.

As for the rest of the folks on West Hackmatack Street, they go about their business dreaming of church socials and town meetings, of fund raising for the new hospice, of the latest mess the school board's made of the high school curriculum. Of deer season and wild turkey shoots, of husbands and wives and lovers and in-laws, of grocery bills and land taxes and the price of a cord of wood.

And if they dream of Windigo or the little people, if they dream of Manitou or the Hidden Folk at all, they awake blessing their new god for keeping such things faraway and long ago.

Not to mention untrue.

For the past three nights, there's been a ring of ice around the moon. And for each of these nights, deep under West Hackmatack Street, down near the otkon *in its lair (which to the untutored eye looks merely like a possum with mange, but to one of sight looks more like a huge blue rodent of malign power), Manitou, tormented by presentiment and pestered with dreams of obvious and irritating allegory, has turned over, sighing in its sleep.*

I'm listening for the sound of her footsteps. The old woman ought to be walking by now. It's two fifteen in the morning and I haven't heard her yet.

Aren't we funny? Somewhere else, I might be worried about a woman I heard walking the corridors at night. Here, I worry that the woman is not walking the corridor. Is she dead in her

23

efficiency unit? Did she choke on her dentures or have a hip give out, and suddenly falling, hit her head on the mantle? We don't have mantles in River House. Maybe she's had a stroke and even now she's lying alone unable to cry out. Much more likely: the local sanitarium netted her—at long last.

I don't worry long though. I am actually writing. Nothing I am entirely sure of, but at least the words finally come. I'm writing my autobiography. Since biographies and autobiographies are the greatest fictions of all, naturally, I'm not telling the truth. Like all autobiographers, I'm creating a myth since myths are the greatest truths of all. Although someone (I can't recall who) once said, "The biggest enemy of truth is not the lie—it's the myth."

Whoever said that has no idea what a myth is. Whoever said that is no artist. Whoever said that believes "facts" are "truths." Idiot. In any case, as a natural born liar, my autobiography is coming rather easily.

There are no footsteps this night. No spider outside my door.

I see her the next afternoon. I am two blocks from River House, on a side street of shops which would all be on Main Street if they could afford the rent. I am here because of the thrift shop. Other than my futon mattress, a cheap summer blanket, a cheap sheet and pillowcase set, a pillow and a bath towel, all found in a factory outlet store on the edge of town, and my seeds and my wine and my notebook from Price Chopper, as well as a box of #2 pencils, I've bought all I've so far needed here. Two wineglasses (I expect no company; the second glass is in case I break the first one), one fork, one table knife, one spoon, a small cooking pot, a bowl.

I'm inspecting a large cup. I hadn't thought I needed a cup, large or otherwise, but this one has caught my eye. Thick buttery yellow with a small rose-red rose almost like cloisonné on its crackled side, it reminds me of something. Perhaps my mother had one like it when I was young? It couldn't have been my father. I don't remember a father. Looking up from the cup on its shelf of mismatched kitchenware, I see her outside the charity shop. She is about four feet away staring at me through the shop's window. This close, I see she has what must be psoriasis. Seeming to grow out from under her damp, limp, colorless hair, angry red scales cover half her low forehead, most of her right cheek. It's begun its attack on her neck and chin.

She is ugly enough without the psoriasis. It's not that her nose is particularly ugly, or her eyes, or her mouth. It's not even that they all sit in her face at slightly the wrong angles: the thin mouth slanting up on one side, down on the other, the left eye, wet and drooping, just that much higher than the right—it's the petulance. It's the stamp all over of sly ill-temper and craven ill-will.

She is younger than I thought. Quite a bit younger. She's not a girl but she's not an old woman either. Fifties? Sixties?

I cannot bear to look at her. I turn away. When I turn back, she is gone.

I really don't need a cup. I put it back.

There's something odd about my closet. Lying

25

here, my laptop on my stomach, a glass of wine on the thin brown carpet by my side, I've been staring at it, not really seeing it. I've been reading a short story from a book of Daphne du Maurier's short stories I brought "home" from the library: *Don't Look Now*, a rotten peach of a tale. All about a husband and wife whose little girl has just drowned.

Looking up from the ill-chosen pages, I see it now. In the corner of my corner room, my closet is too big. I mean, inside—there's too much of it. I don't understand how there can be so much inside what is so small outside. I get up, cross the room on my bare feet, look inside. I'm right. The inside of my closet is much larger than it has a right or reason to be. I tap the wall. What would a hollow wall sound like? I keep tapping in the hopes of finding out. Sounds like me tapping a wall. It hurts my knuckles.

I should get back to work. I'm no longer writing an autobiography. I've bored myself into a complete impasse. Besides, I find myself turning again and again to the woman, to the girl, who can't keep still. I find myself constructing a story around her. It's turning into a mystery, perhaps even a ghost story...which suits my mood—and River House. Now that I live here, now that I call it home, River House doesn't seem quite as ordinary anymore. It's not a palace. It hasn't been a palace for a long time. It's not a hotel. What is it?

I'm not sure what I think about this question.

I'm right. There is something not quite kosher about my closet. I push my clothes out of the way, a matter of a single second's effort. Aside from the

usual overhead shelf on which I've piled the few
things that would ordinarily go into a dresser, there
is a low shelf in the back, more like a step, rising a
foot from the closet floor. I've placed my shoes on
this step shelf: a pair of black pumps with modest
high heels, sturdy brown walking shoes, an old pair
of black tennis shoes. The sandals I wear daily
are left on the floor. Pushed to one side are my
laptop case and the large leather bag. The leather
bag is unpacked, or at least most of it is. What's
still inside it, is locked inside it. I pull out both the
case and the bag; take the shoes from the shelf.

What is it about my closet that troubles me?

This is nuts. I know what I'm doing. I'm doing
anything to avoid doing what I ought to be doing.
Writing what is no doubt my last book. Turning
back to my screen, I suddenly remember what
some other writer said somewhere, and feel a sour
grin tug at my mouth. "Nobody ever committed
suicide while reading a good book," said he, or
maybe she, "but many have while trying to write
one."

Something wakes me up. A loud pounding.
How long has it been going on? Is it at my door? Is
there something wrong?

I suddenly realize—my god, the building's on
fire! I can't do another fire. I can't feel another
fire. Someone is warning me, warning the others
who live here. I leap up from my futon bed. Not
bothering with what I wear, what I look like, what
time it could be, not even pausing to turn on the
light, I am across the darkened room in one jump.
My mind is filled with fire.

27

Whoever is pounding, pounds louder. I hear you. I'm coming. Don't leave me!

Terrified, I fumble with the door latch. My fingers are stupid with fear; what should take less than a moment takes an eternity.

I finally throw open my door.

Nothing. There is no one out here, no one pounding on my door or on anyone else's door. No other door is open. No one else, crazed by the fear of fire and a pounding in the night, stands as I do, bedazzled by an empty corridor.

The pounding comes again. Only once, a single tremendous blow. As if a wrecker's ball has finally found River House.

It's not my door. It's in the closet.

I whirl round to face it. And behind me, the door to my room slams shut. I am in the dark once more.

As ever, I am amazed by the writer's mind. I begin a book about myself and the world dissolves into only me. A ghost story begins to take place under my hand, and the world is haunted. Perhaps I shouldn't read my library books. Or write a ghost story. I am already haunted. I'm not sure I could take more of it.

I drink myself back to sleep. Again.

A month ago, I lived in Malibu by the sea. One month ago I had no idea I was close to death—mine or anyone else's. Not dying meant I was still trying to live, and living was becoming more difficult by the hour. By no intention of my own, I'd stumbled into the movie business. It happens when you're a writer and somebody thinks something you've written might do them some good, open a door, make them a movie.

The movie business is like a small town, smaller than the town of Little Sokoki where no one knows my name. In the movie business, everyone knows your name. Or at least your "product." They know what you do because what you do might have something to do with them. They know if you're going up or coming down. If you're going up, you can't move for all the friends who surround you. If you're going down—what friends?

Few places are stranger than Malibu. In it live more world famous people than any other town on earth. Real estate per week can cost as much as many earn in a year. Yet it's a dump. Bisected by the bumper-to-bumper Pacific Coast Highway, its beaches are filthy, its stores shabby, its layout shambolic. The carpet in the library was new when Gidget was surfing. There's a center of sorts: a large, flat, and very vacant lot edged by a cold sea and hot hills. All of it is forever burning up or sliding down.

I imagine the rich and famous like it that way. It discourages the poor and obscure from hanging around.

For four years, he and I lived in a very nice house up a scrubby canyon above the "town" of Malibu, very near the rehab center where half of Hollywood gets sent when the police catch up with them. For three years Kate lived with us, not counting her time in my womb. All four of those years I shamed myself by writing to order. That's what he said: "shamed myself." He also said: "writing to order." He, meanwhile, accepted work if he felt like it, drank if he felt like it. He felt like

drinking more than he felt like working. He drank
to forget he was dying. We all die, even movie stars.
But he thought he was dying sooner than the
usual span of time because great artists die young.
In any case, whenever he sobered up, there was
always a part for him. A good part. A very good
part. Because he was good. Because there was no
one else like him.

It went on like that right up until the day of the
fire.

He might have been right. I suppose I was filled
with shame. But if I was, I was too numb to feel it.

I'm back in Price Chopper, idling along an aisle
of wines. French, Californian, Spanish, Italian,
German, even Vermont wines. I skip the Vermont,
go for the German whites. Red wine hurts my
head. Vermont wine is too delicate, too fruity, too
politically correct. I read every label. It seems
Vermont hasn't discovered grapes. Right next
to the ports and the sherries hangs a display of
batteries. Why here? Then again, why not? To sell
the batteries, there's an offer of a cheap flashlight.
I didn't need a cup, but I'm sure I need a flashlight.
All good ghost stories require a good flashlight.

I buy three bottles of wine and one flashlight.
With extra batteries.

In the library there's a book about Little Sokoki,
written by various members of the Little Sokoki
Historical Society. It can't be checked out so I've
read parts of it in a big soft chair in the library's
front window. River House has half a chapter to
itself. And three black and white photographs.
One was taken at its completion. (I am saddened

to see there was once a second-floor iron balcony running the length of Main Street. A splendid thing. Why was it removed? Where did it go?) A second photo taken in the year 1927 (the balcony is still there), and a third sometime in the Seventies. In each photo, aside from the third where the balcony has mysteriously vanished, River House looks just as it does now. All around it, Little Sokoki grows up and falls down, horses and tram lines disappear, the cars and the clothes change with the years, trees are planted and then uprooted, then planted again, faces come and go, but River House remains the same.

My hotel is one hundred and forty-four years old. Planned and paid for by Charles River Akeley, it was a monument to himself. Born in Little Sokoki in 1821, a failure in school, in employment, and in love, Charles fled to the hills of California and somehow inveigled a fortune from his fellow gold seekers. River House, erected some years later, said all C.R. Akeley needed to say to Little Sokoki.

I am astonished to learn who has stayed here. Or merely wandered through. Among them: Henry Wadsworth Longfellow, Rudyard Kipling, Mary Baker Eddy, H.P. Lovecraft, Harry Houdini, Louise Brooks, Alfred Hitchcock just before filming *The Trouble With Harry*, Shirley Jackson, who lived and died forty miles away in North Bennington, Vermont, doing a rare, forced, and terrified interview at the publication of *We Have Always Lived In The Castle*, Stephen King passing through as he wrote *The Stand*...and now—me.

The flashlight is a big help. With it, I can now see into the far back corners of my closet. Of course, there's a loose board. I should have known there would be. When a hotel is one hundred and forty-four years old, when forty years ago it was slated for demolition, but saved at the last moment by a property speculator, when Hitchcock, Houdini, and Lovecraft have walked its halls, not to mention Jackson and possibly King, it's bound to have a few nooks and crannies that didn't, or wouldn't, fit in with the remodeling plans. Curious, I pull at the board. With a little effort, and some kind of tool, I think I can pry it free. Table knife's no good. Too small. Too flimsy. But I won't use the bigger better one even if it was up to the job. And I can't ask my unknown neighbors. "Excuse me, but you wouldn't happen to have a handy crowbar I could borrow, would you?"

It seems I'll be unlocking my leather bag again. A woman needs her hammer.

Watching a coven of the Little Sokoki homeless at twilight, I'm sitting in a pocket park at the end of Main Street near the bridge over the river. Like rats, they've crept out from their cardboard dens in the green tangle of the riverbank, are probing the trash cans. Like pigeons, they peck at the refuse.

I watch, remembering the homeless in Santa Monica. So many on the semi-tropical streets, if you gave each one a buck as you walked the few blocks from Lincoln to the sea, you'd be lucky to wind up with change from a hundred dollar bill. I remember asking him: what does it take to sleep in pissy doorways, to scrounge through slimed dumpsters, to beg in our new America? They can't all be the institutionalized thrown out of their cozy institutions, or runaway American kids shooting up the Hollywood dream. They can't all be latter-day *My Man Godfreys*. Somewhere along the way, they made choices. Even the ignorant, the oppressed, the afflicted, the innocent, and the stupid make choices.

If whatever happened to them, happened to us, I said, looking out over our unnaturally green back garden in the yellow Malibu hills, what choice would we make?

He said if he had a camper, he'd do what William Shatner did after *Star Trek* got cancelled. Live in it with his dog. But without a camper or a dog, he'd hang out in rich people's back yards. Eat their pet's food. Take baths in their heated pools. Sleep in their cabanas. Crap in their exotic flower beds. Eventually someone would rediscover him, and when they did, they'd give him a job. He was, after all, a genius.

He was kidding. But not entirely.

I said I'd like to think I would walk away. That I would seek what's left of the Wilderness and take my chances alone like that kid, McCandless I think his name was, who wandered off into Alaska, only to die in an old abandoned bus from eating the wrong wild thing growing in the Alaskan woods. Or better yet, mysteriously disappear into the desert wilderness like that wonderful boy back in 1934. Everett Ruess walked away one day, and from that moment to this has never returned, or left sign of his passing...except to carve one word on a rockface. The word was *Nemo*, which in Latin means "no one." What I actually did was write a book, then a screenplay, based on what I hoped I'd have the moxie to do. It made a much better movie than it did a book; it was much better starring

33

Susan Sarandon than me. For one thing, until a month ago I never really walked away. No getting round it—when my time came, I ran.

Still. I want to think I am not a rat or a pigeon or a dog eating dog food. I want to think I'm a cat, not so much running, as prowling.

What I've actually done is gone to ground. Like a rabbit.

She's here. Standing just behind a fellow in rags stiff with filth. He's sniffing at something he's found in the trash. Now he nibbles at it. He ignores her, or hasn't yet noticed her. I watch her watching him. He seems to fascinate her. She has begun to fascinate me. What is she doing besides getting smaller, flake by flake? Who is she? Outside, by the light of the dimming day, she looks younger than she did through the window of the thrift shop. Younger and smaller. But no cleaner.

Oh hell. She's seen me. She's turning my way.

I get up and hurry off. The thought of her standing as near to me as she stands to the ratman dining off trash disgusts me. And, somehow, also frightens me.

My hammer weighs down my bag.

Because he once stayed here, I've checked out a collection of stories by H.P. Lovecraft. A blurb on the back cover informs me that Lovecraft should not be read alone, and never after dark. But I am alone. It's just gone midnight and I'm sipping wine and reading *The Whisperer in Darkness*. It's set only a few miles from here. Nearby towns are mentioned, roads I've traveled, rivers I've sat beside, woods I've wandered in. He calls Vermont a "region half-bewitched."

I wonder which room was his. I wonder if he wrote this particular story of alien possession in it. River House was still a hotel then. Its ceilings were still high, its walls "unfeatured." I've seen photos. The walls were papered in flowers. In birds. In creeping vines. There were no closets; there were only wardrobes. All the beds were four-poster beds. A man who seemed not to notice his own times, I wonder if Lovecraft foresaw the shame that would come to River House.

I stop reading and go back to prying the loose board away from the wall in the back of my closet.

It comes all of a sudden—so suddenly, I fall backward, almost smacking myself in the forehead with the head of the hammer. I'm lying on my back, catching my breath, thanking my lucky stars (now, there's a laugh), in short, doing anything and everything but noticing what I've uncovered. When I do notice, I almost fall over again, this time from wonder.

Behind the wall are stairs.

Well, of course there would be stairs, it's only fitting. There's something that lives in a writer making all this stuff up. And whatever or whoever that something is lives deep down in the brain, somewhere even the writer herself cannot see. Stephen King laid it right out there. He said he was so drunk and so coked out tapping away at his stories, he doesn't even remember writing them. If he didn't, who did? The thing living deep down inside, that's who. Or what. The something that only whispers through my laptop while the rest of me is dying for a pee or a tuna melt.

It takes me what remains of the night to make a hole large enough to crawl through.

By then I'm too tired—and to be honest—
too tipsy, to bother. Destroying a wall is an
exhausting, messy, business. I shower, and fall
into bed.

What time is it? By the light in my window,
the one looking down onto Main Street and across
to another red brick building that separates me
from the sweet green face of the river, it's late in the
afternoon. I've forgotten I own a traveling clock. I
dig it out of a side pocket in my laptop case, set it
by the clock face in the church steeple next to the
library.

I am wasting the little time I've given myself. I
am meant to be writing a book. I am meant to be
trying not to die.

I sit up a bit, push my ratted hair out of my
eyes, scooch back into my pillow. I switch on my
laptop, place it on my stomach, wait for it to boot
up. Listening to the busy sound it makes, my eyes
alight on the hammer lying on the carpet in front of
the bathroom door. Oh fuck. It comes back to me.
I've made a hole in my apartment wall big enough
to drag a small couch through. If I had a couch.
What in the world was I thinking? I do not own this
apartment. I could be asked to leave. I could be
evicted. Then where would I be? I've spent a large
part of my remaining money on the first and last
month's rent. Covering the security deposit. I'm
not sure my security deposit is enough to cover the
cost of repairing the wall.

Why would I destroy the wall? Is it the drink?

Surprised and horrified, I allow myself to look
at my closet. Plaster and lathe dust are ground
into the carpet. Splintered boards lean against the

closet door, scattered chunks of masonry litter the
floor. My mind chatters at me: if I cleaned up; if I
got rid of the residue; if the closet door were closed,
would anyone notice?

From now on, I'll keep it shut. Besides, no one
ever comes in here. This isn't a real hotel; there
are no maids, no room service. And I've covered my
trail well enough. No one knows where I am. Not
yet, anyway. If they did, they'd be here. And if, for
some reason, someone from Little Sokoki should
knock, I would not let them in. As for leaving, if I
leave, how long before the management found out?
Long enough. Besides, if I wind up dead, they can
sue me. I find this last thought comforting.

An hour later, I am driven out by hunger.

It's gone dark by the time I walk home. It's that
still hour after the shops have closed and before
people come out for the evening. There's no one
in the parking lot behind River House and off High
Street but me. I stop under a sodium mercury
lamp, stare up at it. It's agig with fireflies. They
flare up as bright as the hiss of a sudden match,
fall like whirligigs, climb again, do loop-de-loops in
the light. Nearby, cat's cradled in the phone wires,
two huge spider webs glutted with the bodies of
the dead, glow by the light of the sodium lamp and
the fireflies. I'm thinking of Anne Sexton. Some
time before she gassed herself in her own garage,
wearing her mother's fur coat with a tumbler of
vodka in hand (it was a glorious October day and
she'd just lunched with a friend and proof-read the
galley sheets of her last book of poems, poems she
sensed weren't "good enough"), she wrote: "I could
admit that I am only a coward crying me me me

and not mention the little gnats, the moths, forced
by circumstance to suck on the electric bulb."

I can admit that too. It's always me. Who else
do I see in the little gnats, the moths?

I move on only when the local children of the
night begin to appear, small town children, pitiful
impersonations of real evil.

With them, yet not with them, stands
the ragged dog who sat by the youth with the
camcorder. His coat is so filthy I can't tell what
color he is. He stares at me as I hurry off.

To make doubly sure no one sees what I have
done to the wall—what if my apartment is inspected
for bugs; what if a fire really were to break out?—I'll
use some of my fallen ceiling tiles to cover the hole
in the back of my closet. They'll stay there if I prop
my big leather bag up against them.

If I knew who to go to, I'd ask about the woman
with psoriasis. Surely, other people in River House
find it strange that she walks the corridors in the
middle of the night, that she sometimes pounds
on doors. I'd try management, but after making a
hole in my closet wall, I don't want to attract their
attention.

Management consists of the dismissive Miss
Jackson who works four days a week in an
office at the far end of High Street's second floor.
Management also consists of the present owner of
River House, the only son of the man who saved it
from the wrecking ball. But the blandly attractive,
mildly avaricious Benjamin Willow comes here
only once a week. Other than Miss Jackson and
Mr. Willow, there's maintenance. Maintenance
is a small furtive man with a dent on the bridge

of his purple nose who lives on the ground floor, tucked away in a tiny apartment behind the movie house and the lingerie shop. He drinks. I know he does. Half the time I'm there, he's there—in Price Chopper's liquor aisle. He also goes to the New Hampshire dog track about twenty miles from here. I've seen his loser's tickets torn and scattered like bread crumbs leading down and down to where he, I suppose, lives.

Right now, I'm cleaning up. I am also, from time to time, glancing at the hole in my closet wall. The stairs in the back of my closet go not only up, but down. Down could end up in *The Last Ditch.* Up might make it all the way into the main tower. This tower, taller than the two at either end of the building, extends at least another thirty feet above the flat roof of the fifth floor. No one lives in the tallest tower. There is no apartment up there. The floor plans of each of River House's five floors show all three towers as blank space. The only difference in the tallest corner tower is that it is more ornate, much larger, and that there is much more blank space.

There's something about all this, something that comes and goes in my mind like the windows of a passing train. I can see in, but can't quite know what I'm looking at. And then I do. I remember. I wrote about this, about holes, about doors. In *The Windigo's Daughter*, Faye, my unlikely heroine, has a door.

I'm back on my bed, hitting keys on my laptop. Calling up old files. I find *The Windigo's Daughter.* I find the door in the first few pages of the book.

Faye on her porch isn't like the other folks
of Wobanaki Falls. Faye is as exotic as a
yeti...though she'd never admit it—not even
if someone with the wit to see the difference
also had the nerve to mention it. For instance,
look what's happening right now. A fly, blue
as an otkon, *big as a boiled sheep's eye,*
buzzes by...stops to hover an inch from her
nose. Her eyes crossed, Faye shoos it away;
it comes back. She shoos it away again,
but it comes back. Its hum and its buzz:
buzzzzuuummmmbuzzzum, almost a tune
and the tune almost has words—the humming
words seem to say: buzzafayebuzzum.

Faye bats it out of the air...and when
the little blue body thumps to the porch, she
squashes it flat with her bare foot. Then kicks
the tiny carcass into the telltale pile of wee
bones and chitinous debris behind the door.

She hates it when that happens. Animals
speaking to her. Animals—and now, not
just dogs and cats and big black and white
cows, but bugs—are forever trying to speak to
Faye. But she won't listen. Instead, she'll get
married and that will be that.

She will wed Mr. Honig, a man lately come
up from the south, the traveling man...yes, she
will—and all the flies in Wobanaki Falls, all
the flies in Vermont, will not stop her. No, they
won't.

Not if she stays away from the two sugar
maple saplings that grow behind her house
on West Hackmatack Street, grow like whips,
like twins, like two thin doorjambs at the edge
of her lawn, many yards past the tent with

the long pink table. Not if she never passes through them or even near them. And she won't. Why should she? So far as it goes, Faye likes Mr. Honig. Another woman might like him more, but Faye isn't another woman. When she marries Mr. Honig, he's promised to take her away from the pleasant and peaceful town of Wobanaki Falls...no fooling around, she's been here long enough. Besides, she has to get out of Vermont—the sooner, the better. They'll travel, Mr. Honig says, he'll take her some places, show her some things. If not for that promise, she'd much rather eat Mr. Honig than wed him.

Enough of that. I know where the sapling door takes Faye. Anyone who saw the movie knows where the sapling door takes my heroine, Faye. My stairs, on the other hand, could only take me up to a tower of blank space. Or down to *The Last Ditch*. Both of these things are too symbolic, even for me.

This is intolerable. It's two fifteen in the morning and she's out there, pounding at my door. I've already told myself that if it happens again, I will not open up. I will ignore it. Confrontation only encourages crazy people. By now I'm sure she's crazy. Why else would she do what she does? There's no logic to it. No purpose. Except perhaps to drive me mad along with her. Not likely. My own life has done for me already. Compared to that, a little pounding in the night is laughable.

I have work to do here.

Tomorrow, hole in the closet wall or no hole in

the closet wall, I will beard Miss Jackson in her lair
and file a complaint.

That did not go well at all. Does this mean
I now have to find Mr. Willow and file another
complaint against Miss Jackson?

Aside from having to actually speak to
someone, the worst part of it was that the
excessively rude Miss Jackson stated firmly, and
without fear of contradiction (most especially by
me), that there is no such person as I've described
living in River House. And no one else has ever
complained about any nocturnal knocking.

As a writer, this is about what I expected. As
what passes for a normal person, I am confused.
As myself, I am unsettled.

If she doesn't live in River House, how does
she get in past six o'clock? At six every evening,
the outer doors electronically lock. After that, and
until eight in the morning, those of us who live
here must use some sort of encoded key card. If
she doesn't live in River House, does she come here
when anyone can wander the corridors, then hide
after the downstairs doors lock. If so, where? If so,
why?

I've lost the thread of my book. In this room
over two weeks now, and all I've succeeded in doing
is making a hole in a wall. I've also managed to
alienate Miss Jackson. Plus, I've scared myself. I
will not be reading any more H.P. Lovecraft.

Complete strangers used to stop us on the
street, most of them hopeful actors. They wanted
to say something to him. They wanted to make him

notice them. They loved what he did, and so they thought he *was* what he did, and that they were like him—or that they could be like him, if only they had the talent or the breaks. Standing aside, giving them room (after all, I was only a writer, an Emily Dickinson "nobody"), it seemed so obvious to me: they imagined that talent was contagious. They hoped they could catch it by loving him, by telling him they loved him. He was flattered, of course. He was also frightened. He thought if they got too close, they'd see him for what he really was—without genius. He was wrong. They would never see him. And he did have genius. What he did not have was sense. I had all the sense. Which he scorned in me. And envied. And used unmercifully.

He called me his Houdini Heart. He thought I hid keys under my tongue. He thought I could dislocate my shoulders. He thought I could hold my breath forever. He thought I could wriggle my way out of anything. He counted on it.

He was wrong about that too. On second thought, maybe he wasn't. So far, now that "anything" has happened, I'm still safe—from everyone but me.

I might be drinking too much. I do know this, I'm doing more drinking than writing, and more sleeping than drinking. I've slept for most of the last two days. This can't go on. I'm not stupid. I've left no paper trail, used no credit cards, contacted no one, kept my head down. My room in River House, my Little Sokoki library card, is under an assumed name. I have no phone, landline or cell, no internet service, no post office box. But they're not stupid either. Well, actually they are. Like most people. But one of them will realize at some point that people always go home. One of them is bound to think of looking here.

I've begun a new book. I've also begun waking with headaches. Have to add aspirin to my Price Chopper list. Maybe it's the wine. Should I drink something else? He used to drink vodka. He used to say how much harm could something do that you could barely see, barely taste, barely smell?

I said: but if it doesn't do any harm, will it do any good? That made him laugh. We used to do that. Laugh.

I saw the beautiful young man in the lobby today, the one with the camcorder. He still had it, slung round his neck on a strap. We waited for the elevator together. I steeled myself, but this time, he did not speak to me. He smiled, once. It was a small smile, nothing I need return. Or cling to. I averted my eyes, stared at the numbers lighting up: Three, then Two, then One. As we waited, I came very close to opening my mouth, asking him about the girl walking the corridors, the one who pounded on doors, but a tall man—all hard angles, windblown hair, beads of gleaming sweat, and an enthusiast's stench—came along, forcing himself and his mountain bike into the elevator. I live on the third floor, silly to take the elevator, even carrying two bottles of vodka, a large package of sunflower seeds, a bottle of generic aspirin, and a gallon carton of orange juice. The door closed on the youth and the bicyclist.

Climbing the stairs, I suddenly felt like her, the woman who doesn't live here.

It's too hot to write. Too hot to sleep. I go down to the riverbank again.

There was once an island in the middle of the wide curving Connecticut. It rose up just where the Blackstone Brook bounces down out of the mountains and plunges into the dark watered river. On it the people of Little Sokoki built a dance pavilion. I saw its photo last week in the book I sat reading in the window of the library. Built a few years after River House, the pavilion was graceful and white, made whiter against the bluegreen of the river water and the deep green of the mountain on the far bank. Small triangular flags flew from its pitched roofs; deep porches shadowed its dancers. The photo was taken in the summer of 1927. Was there one among them—the girl with her head thrown back, laughing; the boy leaning far over the rail—who somehow sensed the pavilion and most of the island would be swept away in the Great Flood of early November in that same year, 1927?

A typical writer's question. A typical writer's ploy. To not only display a delicacy of feeling, but to foreshadow the plot. Oh! the attentive reader is meant to ask (hopefully with a delicious shiver), is someone going to die in the river's soon-to-be rising waters?

Kafka wrote (Christ, the stuff I can pull from my brain now I'm about to extinguish its little warblings forever): "The books we need are the kind that act upon us like a misfortune, that make us suffer like the death of someone we love more than ourselves, that make us feel as though we were on the verge of suicide, or lost in a forest remote from all human habitation—a book should serve as an axe for the frozen sea within us."

Tasty line:...*serve as an axe for the frozen sea within us.* But I still resent Franz Kafka. It's hard enough to write at all, but to write something we need? Heaven help me. Heaven help all writers.

The island is still here, but only enough of it to anchor the bridge that leaps from Vermont to New Hampshire in two arched and aging spans.

As on my first day here, I cross only the Vermont bridge, climb down its steep cement sides to sit on the diminished island.

The fish is gone. Not even its bones mark where it lay, dead in the toxic air. I make a nest for myself in the fine brown sand and the fiddlehead fern. No one could see me here. But I can see them. Little Sokoki goes about its business atop the green bank on the Vermont side. The homeless go about theirs in the jungled bank. As it has always done, the white frothed Blackstone leaps out from the rocks, vanishes into the slowly sweeping river waters. Behind buildings a century old, some quite a bit older, there is a crane as high as a church steeple swaying over a side street. They are constructing a multi-story parking lot in Little Sokoki. It will be the paste jewel of Maple Street. I am sure the merchants are glad to have it. I am sad to know they need it. I should like Little Sokoki to stay as it is. No, not as it is. As it was. I should like it to be as it was when River House was a palace. I should like to be the little girl who saw it like that.

There's the roof of River House with its three towers. The central and tallest tower sits two stories above my one small room, a room I cannot see from here. Each tower is windowed on all four sides: four high windows, all rounded at the top. But the central tower, the one like an enormous pawn piece, is set at an angle so that its larger windows face precisely west and east, south and north. The maintenance man is shorter than I am. I'll bet he's drunker. Wager anything those windows haven't been washed in years.

Writers live their stories. I've come close to commitment in a state asylum, served as a maid to a British bitch, been punched in the face by a jealous wife on an Indian Reservation, worked as a stringer on a large New York newspaper back when New York had newspapers. I've exercised racehorses and raced motorcycles. Once, scared out of my wits, I wormed my way through a black rocky tube deep under the city of Glastonbury. For *The White Bee* I lived in the dead of winter for an entire month in the far north of Finland, just me and a herd of reindeer and people smothered in endangered fur. For my screenplay of a middle-aged middle-class woman who'd walked away from Middle America to die, I spent three days and two nights alone in the Sonoran Desert with a very cranky burro.

What kind of story am I living now? Dozing and dreaming on the riverbank on a sunny afternoon, I'm Alice. Falling down holes.

I was born in New York City. My mother told me that. If she hadn't told me, I would never have

known. But she could have been lying. She lied
to make her own life worth living. What she made
of my life by her lies is still a maze to me. Maybe
I wasn't born in New York City at all. Maybe I
wasn't even hers. I don't look like her. I don't
think like her. We had nothing in common except
her lies. All I really know is what I remember and
I remember so little. I know this: we lived in small
towns, one after the other. Sometimes she rented
a room; sometimes, if the local pickings were good,
a whole apartment. My mother liked men. God
knows why since the ones she met were losers.
Even a little kid could tell they were wastes of
space, so what she saw in them beats me. A meal
ticket? Forget it. Some of them were married, a
few held jobs, but not one of them ever had money.
A laugh? I don't think so. They weren't all grim,
and one or two weren't exactly stupid, but no one
was smart and no one was funny. When it came
right down to it, I think they were company, warm
bodies in the middle of the night. And someone to
drink with.

I'm making my mother sound like a drunk. I've
always thought of her as a lush. Lush is an old-
fashioned word. There's something sad about it,
something softly rotten.

I'm also making her sound like a hooker. She
was never a hooker. Men didn't give her money;
she gave it to them—which is why she and I never
had any. My mother worked hard for a living.
Any old job would do. She drove a taxi in Marin
County, California. Somewhere in Washington
state, she waitressed for HoJos. For the three years
we lived in Vermont, she worked as a cashier in the
Grand Union grocery store. Taxis and restaurants

and grocery stores are good places to meet needy men. And needy men were why we always had to leave town. A wife would chase her away, or she'd lose the apartment when she couldn't pay the rent, or she'd follow some guy to a new life in a new town, where it would always be just like the old life in the last town.

Me? I went along for the ride. Always the nervous left-out new kid, I went to school a year here, a year there. I read a lot of books when the town had a library, saw a lot of movies when she wanted me out for the afternoon, missed a lot of meals when money was tight, dug deep holes in the woods when the soil was soft and sat in them, hiding the day away, and sometimes even the night. I endured a lot of men. Maybe I've conveniently forgotten, but I don't recall a single one of them hitting on me. Later, when I heard stories like that, so many sad and nasty stories told in so many ways, I had nothing to relate to. The men my mother chose to spend her money on, liked her, not me. That was probably her single criteria: they liked her. Odd, now that I think of it. Odd that I was no one's Lolita. Am I saying I should have been? Or am I saying I wanted to be—wanted? What I hope I'm saying is that my mother chose well for me, but badly for herself.

She died on the job. Nothing like an accident, or driving the wrong person at the wrong time. She just blinked out one day sitting in a San Rafael taxi loading zone behind the wheel of her cab. They found her there, still sitting, still breathing, but gone. It took a week for her body to follow on after. Her last man, something called Rudy who ran the projector in a movie house in another Marin County town, hawked everything she owned.

I was sixteen years old.

I come awake with a jump start. I'm back behind my eyes, fingers digging into the muddy sand of the riverbank, my blood as carbonated as soda water, my heart hot in my throat.

For some reason, I'm shuddering in my skin. Nothing's changed. The river still flows by inches from my feet. The sun still shines. I'm still hot. But I glance across the river towards River House— where its tower windows will be as they've been since I got here: blank, unwashed, empty.

Sweet Jesus. If not my imagined mother, who then stands on the inside ledge of the east window of the tallest tower?

The elevator, not under the corner tower, ascends only to the fifth floor. The stairs, across the hall from the elevator, can also only be climbed to the fifth floor. There is no utility apartment up here, no apartment at all directly under the largest tower with the largest windows. But there is a ballroom.

I've snuck in. It's not Benjamin Willow's one day at work although it is a day of toil for Miss Jackson. Before breaking into the ballroom, I'd made sure she'd gone to lunch in that little sandwich shop and bakery on Main she favors; that the maintenance man was down on the fourth floor fixing someone's toilet in the High Street wing. Being the kind of maintenance man he is, the toilet might never get fixed and the storage-ballroom is not always locked.

When River House was young, dancers danced

in this ballroom before ever they danced in the
white pavilion on the island in the river. Now the
huge corner ballroom on the fifth floor—a chevron
as my room is a chevron, but much larger—serves
as storage space. Tables and chairs, old bureaus,
trunks and suitcases, paint cans, drop-cloths,
spare kitchen sinks, old toilets, doorknobs, leftovers
and cast-offs—the remnants of past refittings
and redoings and refurbishings and rearrangings
crowd the walls, litter the sprung wood floor, climb
halfway to the high ceiling with its wedding cake
trim.

All this is the debris of forty something years of
tenants. Here there might even be castoffs and lost
property of over a hundred years of hotel guests.

They haven't lowered the ceiling. It's still up
there, fifteen feet above my head, painted a once
creamy white. Fat little cupids, pink-cheeked and
smirking, stare down through garlands of green
leaves and pink and yellow flowers. The twelve foot
tall windows, once flung open for air when great
balls brightened the room, are sealed shut. I think
that here people laughed, people danced, people
said things that did not matter.

Meanwhile, I've looked everywhere. There are
no stairs from the ballroom up to the tower. There
is no closet, large or small, positioned over my
closet two floors below, to conceal an old staircase.
There's no repair to the ceiling indicating an
opening long sealed off.

I don't understand. Do the stairs in the back of
my closet go only up to the fourth floor? How does
anyone get up to the tower? Once it was built, did
anyone ever go up to the tower?

If there is no way into the tower, how could someone who looked like my mother have been up there? (Certainly not my actual mother who's been dead for at least twenty years; I wasn't there when it happened, didn't hear of her death for some time, so don't actually know when she lied her last lie.) Am I making another mistake, the same mistake I made when I thought I'd seen someone in my own window?

There must be a way into the tower.

I sat in the pocket park again today. Watched the furtively defiant kids, each a perfect clone of street cred, share a joint. Listened to two shaggy men compare the free food program of the Congregationalist Church to the free lunches dished out by the Baptists. So far, I've resisted bringing any booze with me. If I ever do, it won't be in a brown paper bag. I once worked in Hollywood. I once won a literary prize. Woody Allen once stared at me with actual longing over a hotdog at a celebrity baseball game at Yankee Stadium. In London, Terence Stamp once gave me a lingering kiss. Richard Brautigan once read me his as yet unpublished *Trout Fishing in America* all through a San Francisco night. Marlon Brando once sat until dawn on a Malibu beach tempting me with talent. I once sat on Dizzy Gillespie's knee while he told me off-color jokes.

And I once found where he hid his bottles, and there I changed wine into water once and once and once upon a time.

When I become a drunk on a bench, I'll use my stainless steel traveler's mug, the one that says "Carmel by the Sea." And I'll be drinking screwdrivers through a bendy straw.

A bee buzzes by my ear. I swat at it, but miss.

Almost three in the morning. I'm in bed and I'm working. This time I'm writing a sad tale of sad times. It's a little bit stark. A little bit gritty. Stark and gritty signals I'm serious. A writer to reckon with. As for sad…sad is always a winner. Not only that, sad is a snap to write. Want to know how easy it is to work on people's heartstrings? This is how. Set up something they have to like: a kid, a dog, a cranky but cute old man, an amiable half-wit, whatever—then kill it. Like life does. In time, life kills everything.

I'd like to think life killed the puppy I had when I was twelve. But I did. I killed him. After my stray kitten had wandered off, I'd won a puppy by drawing his likeness from a kid's TV show that cleverly saved dogs from the pound by making them prizes in drawing contests. I'd named him Prince. Actually, the name I gave him was longer than that, but out of respect for my long lost dog, I'll keep the rest of it to myself. When I rode my bike, he'd race behind, a bundle of black with lolling tongue and bright eyes. I knew he'd do that, was proud of him for it, yet one day I turned onto a street with too much traffic. I knew it had too many cars, I knew he would follow no matter where I went, yet still I made that turn. The man who hit my dog drove us to the nearest vet, and he did it fast. All the way I cradled Prince in my arms, sobbing. "Don't die," I whispered to him, "don't die." But he did. And when he did, his poor little body gave up such a sickening gassy smell, I gagged. I cried out for him for months.

Whoops. Almost spilled my drink. What you get from using your tummy as a table. Anyway, sad gets the prize every time. Oscar only goes to tales of woe.

Now, funny is hard. Funny is much harder than sad. To make people laugh takes real talent. Like laughing itself. Real laughter is a rare talent. He had it. He could laugh. He could make people laugh. He made me laugh.

I think I'm drunk. No. I know I'm drunk.

Ironic as hell, this. Before the end, I rarely drank. But he was almost always drunk. Being a drunk defined him. It defined who we were. It defined what happened to us. And here I am now, all that's left, still defining away.

Us writers are full of quotes. We quote everybody. If we get desperate enough we quote ourselves and hope nobody will notice we've used the line before. So anyway, Bertrand Russell said: "Drunkenness is temporary suicide." He said more than that, but that little bit's not bad for an old crank like Bertie. A year after meeting and marrying my favorite movie star, I could have come up with the same thought myself.

What's that? Is someone at the door? Is she out there again? I turn my head, listen for a moment. G'way. Got no time for mad people walking at night. Got sad stuff to do here.

Knew I had a headache long before I awoke. Headache was part of my dream. Dream was about an old house, lots of misshapen rooms, up and down stairs, looking for something. I often dream of old houses, strange rooms. Though they are

56

always different, they're all the same: somewhere
I once lived, somewhere I think I've long forgotten.
In them, I am always trespassing. Moving from
room to room, I'm always looking for something or
someone so precious, I weep with loss.

I reach out for the aspirin before I reach for
my laptop, take four with what's left in the glass
by the side of my bed. Then I reach for my laptop.
Meaning to begin again where I left off, I'll read my
stark and gritty sad new book. One paragraph,
two, three—I shudder right down to the curled
bones in my toes.

It's crap. Another night of writing crap.

He once threw a box of his own videos out
a Manhattan hotel window. Then he threw out
the DVDs. Every movie he ever made landed in
duplicate on West 23rd Street with a hideous series
of cracks. That time he was lucky. That time, no
one died.

Even writing crap, I don't think I'm ready to
throw my laptop out a window. But I might throw
me.

It's still dark. What time is it? A little after
four. Four fourteen in the morning. River House
sleeps all around me. Wherever her home might
be, the girl who walks alone must be sleeping as
well. Or if not, she walks alone elsewhere. Nothing
happening below my window. Little Sokoki has
finally gone home, whether home be house or car
or cardboard box. No one drives along Main Street.
Nothing's going up or down High, or on any of the
small side streets. At least not those I can see,
and I can see quite a few of them. No plane passes
overhead full of silently terrified passengers. There

is no sound at all.

Except me, breathing in the dark.

I sit in my bed on the floor, propped up against a wall by pillows. All that lights my room is the computer screen, now showing my screen saver. Nothing personal, something straight out of the Microsoft desktop selection: points of light passing like stars at warp speed. Yet I can see into my closet as if it were day. For some reason, this does not strike me as strange.

I fall asleep like that, sitting up in bed.

Open my eyes who knows how long later, and it is still dark, still quiet. I still have a headache. What time is it? Fourteen minutes after four in the morning.

I won't fix the clock. Who really needs to know what time it is?

When I open my eyes a third time, it's four fourteen. My closet door is closed.

Need more aspirin. Need to pee. Need to pee desperately. Probably throw up as well. Crawl to the bathroom on my hands and knees by the light of my computer's starry screen. Embrace the toilet bowl, staring down into its dark open mouth, my mouth open too. God. Life is hell. There is no hell but life.

Whatever time it actually is, morning is not broken. It's not even hanging by a snagged nail. No pale light washes the shoulders of the unseen mountain rising from the eastern side of the river. New Hampshire's mountain that was once the Sokoki Indian's mountain that always was and ever will be its own mountain, is darker now than it was

58

an hour ago. It's darker outside than it is inside, and the outside dark has a slant and a weight to it that could shatter the glass of my window. I don't mean to, but I lean away.

For more light, I call up the file of the crappy book I've been working on, the bad sad one. Nothing comes up on my screen but—

CHAPTER ONE

I must have deleted my latest mess. I don't remember deleting it.

When I open my eyes again, it is ten minutes after eight. At night? In the morning? Whichever it is, it's still dark.

It's dark. Still dark.

I am a crudely made thing. I have no feeling for feelings. All I have are words. All I can see are primary colors. I get lost in rainbows.

Suddenly, I'm terrified. There is nothing wrong with my clock. There is something wrong with me. Something wrong with my room. There is something very wrong about the dark inside my room, outside my room.

Here's what's worse than never writing my first, my only, good book—what if the sun never dawns? What if the dark is all that's left? I am struck by the most primitive fear of all, the one that begat all those religions we're still stuck with: no light.

But there's light in the closet. I can see it through the door that was open, then closed, and is now open again.

Panicked, I've scrambled off my bed, thrown myself headlong across the floor. By instant dumb instinct, I've crawled into the closet. Like a child would. Like early woman or man would. Like anyone would when face to face with a world gone dark. To hide. To have walls close around me when life grows too large to bear. Seeking light. As all things seek light. Except bats and rats. And, of course, vampires—the foolish overheated creations of those who would live forever. I understand the longing to live forever—but in the same body, as the same person, doing the same bloody thing?

I find my hammer. I'd left it on the floor of the closet when I'd cleared up the mess. I pick it up. A little light and a good hammer. What else could anyone need?

The day it all ended, something had suddenly come up, a producer's meeting, an agent's business lunch, something vitally "important"—no time to find a sitter. Besides, her father was home. So I left her there, with her father.

Kate was three years old and she died. He did not die. Not that day. He died five weeks later. So he was right after all. He died young. Not as young as a "real" artist, but young enough.

In the closet, I can see his face. My hand tightens around the hammer.

I am no longer drunk. I wish I were. If I were drunk I could rule out that I've gone insane. Peering out from the closet into my room, I can see that it is still dark. Has the world come to an end? If it has, has anyone else noticed? Or is it just my world, my version of reality that's stopped? I cannot leave the closet. Out there someone's world has turned its face away. In here, the light still shines. It's coming from behind my suitcase, shining through the hole I made in the closet wall. In here, even over the thud of my relentless heart, I slowly realize I hear music. Faint and distant music. Is it coming from the apartment next door? Do I still have neighbors? I don't know; I've never seen them. But I always know when they're home. When they're home the television is never off. It goes on and on and on and on, beginning first thing in the morning and straight on through to late at night. And to think I wrote some of what I hear through the walls. TV is like a drip feed: drip drip dripping into the brains of my fellow man like sugared water—feeding nothing, but causing all sorts of interesting illnesses. If I could feel, I'd feel ashamed.

The music is sweet, melodic, nothing like the hostile noise that thumps from passing cars or shouts abuse from behind open windows. It sounds like Cole Porter when he was young and his music was young and it's coming from somewhere behind my closet.

It's coming from the stairs behind the closet wall.

I move my leather bag, remove the plastic ceiling tiles; expose the hole I've made in River House. The light and the music tumble out.

Holding my hammer, my hand slick with sweat, I climb through the hole and onto the stairs.

Up and up and round and round. Behind my closet, the stairs are circular stairs, and perhaps they once stood away from the inner wall of River House. But now they are inside the walls, and they wind up and up and up. And as I climb I remember

Faye and my own *The Windigo's Daughter.*

Faye sights along her taut slingshot. A bird, a chipmunk, a cat: anything will do.
Here comes a bee. Now what?
"Buzzzzzzafayebuzzzzaway," says the bee, as ordinary as any ordinary bee—except perhaps for the tiny voice. And the fury behind it. But Faye has already left the porch and is slamming her door.
It's later now. Faye hurries to the church on Cherry Street in her blood-red wedding gown. The wedding guests are surprised. Naturally, they had expected a bride—pure or not—to appear in driven white. (On the other hand, they whisper each to each, in modern times, in times such as these, who can be called pure...and what does purity signify anyway? Such an old fashioned word.) But Faye does not like white. It reminds her of snow and snow reminds her of the cold and cold reminds her of caves and caves remind her of...why go on? The dress is red because red is Faye's favorite color.
The first thing Faye does when she arrives at the church is to go round checking the sash windows. She asks an usher: are they closed? Every one of them? And the doors? Are there any cracks in the walls, open venting, grillwork? She explains that outside a chill has sprung up...but there is no chill.
Faye's guests—all of them her neighbors on West Hackmatack Street or from the bigger houses farther north on Hackmatack

*Common or the folks from the shops where
she buys what little she ever buys—turn in
their polished seats once they've got over
Faye's red dress and Faye's inspection of
the windows and doors. (After all, everyone
agrees, a bride often acts in mysterious ways:
it's a case of wedding day jitters.) But where
is Mr. Honig? And what will he be wearing?*

    *Mr. Honig isn't here yet. Where is the
groom?*

    *A slow buzz, almost like the murmur of
bees, hums through the wedding guests.
What if Mr. Honig doesn't come?*

    *Faye has thought of this too...but
dismissed it. Mr. Honig will come. He knows
better than that.*

It's bright in here, lit by what seems a naked
two hundred watt bulb somewhere far above my
head. And I'm not wearing red and there is no Mr.
Honig. But there is someone singing Cole Porter's
Love for Sale and I think it comes from a stereo or
perhaps a radio, turned low so that no one else is
disturbed in the night. Except me.

    Words reach me now. *Love for sale/Appetizing
young love for sale/If you want to buy my wares/
Follow me and climb the stairs/Love for sale.*

    I laugh softly to myself, at the irony of it, laugh
that my life is full of irony in the last of my days.
He'd think it was funny that not only have I gone
mad before I died, but I'm also providing the music.

    But the real hell of it is, even if I'm no longer
sane, I can still be terrified. I say to myself: this
is a musical dream. A dream musical. In movies,

moments like this moment are almost always
dreams. In dreams, like movies, anything might
happen and we can remain whole. Sane. Safe.
In dreams, we are strong enough to experience
anything at all. It's only in waking life we demand
order: gravity, time ticking by, cause generating
effect, consistency. Or, all else failing, any kind
of order, no matter how nuts. Like our religions.
Now, there's crazy. Imposing our childish need for
Daddy, our childish terror of Daddy, on the cosmos.
(And where's Mommy? Did Daddy kill her?) In
waking life, most of us are not only cowards, we're
out of our minds. He was. I am.

In the hope that I am dreaming, I climb the
stairs.

I open my eyes. It is seven minutes after two in
the afternoon and my window is painted with sun.
My headache is no longer merely a headache, it's
an abomination. I look down the long stretch of my
arm lying outside my covers. My hammer is there,
in my hand. I'm holding my hammer. Dropping
it as I'd drop a snake, I crawl away from my bed,
barely able to raise my head. But I have to find
out. The closet door is open. My leather bag is
pulled away from the hole in the wall. Ceiling tiles
are tossed every which way. The stairs behind the
wall at the back of my closet are not spiral; they are
narrow steps going up at an angle along the inside
of the outside wall. Taking courage, I stick my head
in the hole, look up. There's nothing to see but
the dirt and the dust of the staircase disappearing
into the rising dark. I look down. Nothing but the
stairs disappearing into the lowering dark.

Drink was his ruin. It looks like it might be mine. I shall stop drinking immediately. If I'm to die, it won't be this way. It's too messy. Too common. Too stupid. And too scary.

On the top floor of the Little Sokoki Library there is a big airy room devoted to the history of Little Sokoki. It's where I found the book I browsed, the one full of old photographs. More framed photographs hang from the walls. Blow-ups of Little Sokoki in the 1860s, early in the Twentieth Century, in the 1950s. People, but not places, gone forever. Under glass are Sokoki Indian arrow heads, yellowing bones, trinkets lost and then found in old farmhouses, bits of this or that early device to milk cows or turn water wheels or render tallow.

Shaky, my head aching, slightly nauseous but freshly showered, I'm sober, and I have a plan. I'm writing a book about River House. I'm a little surprised I didn't think of it before. But here I am now, looking for its original architectural designs.

The only person in the room besides me is a fat man at a corner desk. There seems no chair under his tremendous ass, no bones in his body. From time to time he peers out at me through tunnels of flesh. He's making sure. For all he knows, I could be someone come here to confuse the files. Or to steal something. Or spill a forbidden drink. Or stick my chewing gum under one of his tables. He makes me feel naughty. As if at any moment I could do something wrong. Something terrible. Something he'd have to blow a police whistle for.

He doesn't know the half of it.

So far, I've found nothing to steal. If there are

architect's drawings of River House still extant, they aren't here. Not even those made by Benjamin's father.

Pushing my chair back from the table, I stand up. Of course! Benjamin's father.

Before I go to see the son of the man who "saved" River House on the one day he "works," I try to make myself presentable. It's not as easy as it was. I still have a nice dress, but I'm thin. The dress hangs on me; my slacks look empty. As for my hair, the Rodeo Drive cut that cost me a third of my monthly River House rent, is shapeless. But if I smooth my hair straight back, I look decent enough. Even innocent.

For an hour, I stand in front of the bathroom mirror, learning to talk again, to shape my face into smiles, to raise my eyebrows with interest, use my hands to show trustworthiness. I imagine myself any one of a dozen actresses I've watched working themselves into a scene.

"Of course, I shall be careful with the plans, Mr. Willow." Or Benjamin? Should I call him Benjamin? "I'll have them back before you know it, Ben. I'm researching for a book I'm writing. Oh, you didn't know I was a writer?" Eyes down, mouth up in a small shy smile. "I've enjoyed some modest success."

And then he'll want to know if I mean to include him in my book. After all, if it's to take place in his building, the one his father redeveloped, the one he does his best to keep the city from destroying with their ordinances and their taxes and their insistence on capping his rents so that Little Sokoki has more low income housing for the low, doesn't

he merit a mention? And I will laugh, just a little,
and hint that it's just possible he might see himself
in any book I write about River House.

But then I think: if I admit I'm a writer, will
it trigger his memory? Will he recognize me from
newspaper photos? Miss Jackson didn't. Or
wouldn't. When she rented to me, Miss Jackson
seemed thoroughly disinterested in anything about
me save my credit report. And when I told her
I never use credit, never had, never would (the
police follow credit card trails like sharks follow
blood in the water), her interest turned to cash.
"Six months in advance, thank you." But perhaps
Mr. Willow is more aware of what's what in the
world? If I tell him I'm a writer, it could remind
him of headlines. Even in Vermont, the death of
an Oscar winning movie star is very big news. And
he was surely that, a movie star. And he had won
the Oscar. He was also a tender dear heart, and a
complete bastard. Plus, he didn't just die as he'd
always expected. He was murdered. Gruesomely.
Which he did not expect.

But if I'm not a writer researching a new book,
why do I want to see the designs of River House?

I'll tell him I'm an architectural historian.

No one brings a little kid to the Oscars. But
he did. Besides bringing me, he brought Kate. Up
for his third best actor award (he lost the first and
second time), he strode through the enormous
portal of the Kodak Theater and then up the red
carpet to the Rotunda with Kate riding high on
his shoulder. I slipped my arm out of his, held
back for a moment, so that I might walk slightly
behind them. Not out of deference, though that

night I certainly felt it (he was so good at his craft, so wonderfully good), but in order to see my little beauty on his shoulders, to see her long curling red hair bouncing down her back, to watch her wide-eyed watching of the crowd, and their surprised and delighted watching of her, and of course, him, the proud father, the brilliant nominee.

I wore a white retro Hollywood gown by Valentino. Kate wore green chiffon to go with her hair, something he'd had an up-and-coming local designer make for her. It doesn't matter what he wore: it was stylish, it fit him, he was sober.

It was our last completely happy moment. We were all dead in less than a month.

Benjamin Willow isn't in his office. No one is in his office.

When I knocked, the door swung open. It'd been slightly ajar, as if the latch hadn't quite caught. So, if he's stepped out for a moment that means at any minute he could be stepping back in.

My back to the small antechamber that exits into the second floor hallway, I stand in his doorway (one door down from Miss Jackson's much smaller office), and I stare. The architectural designs of River House are on the wall to the right of his desk. Preserved behind glass, they hang just far enough away so that from the doorway I can see them, but I can't see them clearly.

I could wait. I could leave and come back another time. Both of these choices mean I have to do a song and dance with a man called Benjamin Willow. Or I could just walk in and have a look. If caught, I get to play the scene as a dizzy dame. I can do that.

Walking quickly across his office, I position myself under the first and largest of the drawings. This is a detailed rendering of the building as seen from Main Street. I am smiling. So odd to feel a smile. I thought I had none left. I smile to see I was not wrong. In the drawing, it's a palace again. It's full of glamour. It's fey. There is the deep balcony of lacy black ironwork that once graced the second floor. There are the black iron pillars at the edge of the sidewalk to hold up the block long balcony. I glance to my left. The second drawing is a floor plan of the original ground floor level. The third is the second floor. And so on. Moving along, I try to find my own apartment, or at least the larger space that my small studio was carved from. I'm looking for the spiral stairs. Or any stairs.

The elevator's coming. I can hear the squeal it makes closing its doors and I suddenly remember myself. I'm trespassing. I don't want to be found here, snooping. I must leave, and I must leave now. Turning, I see a corkboard mounted on the wall behind Benjamin's large untidy desk. It's pegged for keys. Duplicate keys to every apartment in River House, keys to the ground floor shops, the laundry rooms, the storage rooms, the movie house, the basement, to Miss Jackson's office, to the office I stand in, the one hung round with the designs of River House. Without thinking once, I snatch a set of both office keys from their pegs and hurry from the room, closing the door. This time it catches.

Just as I disappear down the stairwell to the lobby on the first floor, I hear the elevator arrive on the second floor. I've made my escape, as they say, in the Nick Charles of time.

A sickening truth has just become clear to
me. It's only gone noon and I want a drink. I'm
standing with my back against my own closed
door, my hand tight on its doorknob just in case
I was seen after all, and someone come after me
to demand an explanation for trespassing, for the
theft of keys, and I'm staring at the bottle of vodka I
left in my sink. It's in the sink because I'd meant to
pour it down the drain. But didn't.

Moving quickly, I tip the bottle so that it falls
over and empties itself.

He could do things like that. Make grand
gestures. He could pour an entire bottle of the
world's most expensive whiskey into the ocean,
smash it against a wall, stand in the shattered
glass howling of release. He could do that because
all along he had another bottle hidden somewhere
fiendish. I couldn't find them all. He knew I
couldn't find them all.

I have no other bottle.

All I have to do now is wait. Benjamin Willow
will leave for another week, get into his dark
blue high-riding SUV and whisk himself away to
wherever it is he lives. Miss Jackson will catch
her small town bus. The maintenance man will
hunker down in his own utility unit and pretend
he isn't home in case something might actually
need maintaining. And I will sneak into Benjamin
Willow's office. A piece of cake. I have the key.

But first, I have to wait for the dark.

I'm down by the river again, crossing the
Vermont bridge, walking along the sandy fringe of
the island. This long hot day is taking forever to

pass. I do not sweat. I never sweat. But my skin is slick and my pulse races in the heat. I will swim. I will swim in the river even though it is full of toothy fish and slimy garbage and broken glass and toxins. I can't see any of these things, but I know they're there, just under the surface.

On the tangled green bank across from the island, the beautiful boy-man sits amongst the nightshade and fire-red sumac. There's a huge block of cracked and stained cement there, part of what underpinned the old bridge, the one that swept away in the flood a long time ago. That's what he's sitting on, the cement block. He has a book in his hand. I don't think he's reading it, I think he's writing in it. It's a journal. Another writer. My god, we get around. By the shape, I think that's his camcorder on the cement beside him. And so is the dog. Nothing like my puppy, nothing like my puppy would have become if he hadn't died thanks to me. (Would my Prince have thanked me? Why do we say that?) Someone (the youth?) has tied a blue kerchief round its neck. From here it looks bigger, tidier, more content. Dog and man sit on the cement block on the bank below Little Sokoki. I have a feeling they're not together. And yet they are. No one can see them from above. Only I can see them, although I can't see the crane which has dominated the rooftops for so long as I've been here. And I can't see the bridge I've just crossed, the one they built to replace the old bridge with its new cement blocks. Or, for that matter, any cars. I should be able to see all these things. I haven't gone that far from the bridge or the road. For this one moment, Little Sokoki looks as it must have done eighty years ago.

The youth seems to find me fascinating. Not good.

The dog also seems to find me fascinating. His ears are pricked forward, his teeth showing. The youth is putting down his journal, is about to pick up his camcorder. Shit.

In cut-offs and a tee shirt, I quickly wade out to above my knees where the water is blue on top, murky tea underneath. Can't see the bottom, but I can feel it. Out here it's not sand, it's mud. Youth and dog must think I'm nuts. Unless they fall in from boats or bank, or are the children of rats, no one swims in the Connecticut. Little Sokoki long ago turned its hard brick back on the river.

Too bad what they think. It's hot. I'm suffering in the heat. But I am not entirely a fool; I keep my mouth shut tight as I dive into the tea colored water. Bending at the waist, and kicking, I push myself under. Something brushes my thigh. I shake another something from my foot. Out here in the deep water, it's colder, and the pull of the river sweeping down to the sea is stronger. Deep underwater now, I stop swimming. Where is the bottom? There is no bottom. The river goes down and down and down.

Like a dead thing, I drift with the current, my mouth closed but my eyes open. Even so, fuck knows what drifts with me.

Coming up fast for air, I pop out of the river like a seal. I'm very close to the Vermont shore. Very close to the tangled bank but much farther downstream than where I started. First thing I see is the youth and dog. They're standing up. They're both staring at me. The youth is holding his camcorder. At this distance, the boy's face, slightly

Slavic, very exotic, a dancer's face, is twisted with...
what? Fear? Horror? Ears pricked forward, front
paws planted deep in river mud, the dog barks.
Over and over.

They must have thought I'd drowned.

No such luck.

I wave. I am not Stevie Smith, a poet who
longed to go exploring, but instead lived out her
quiet English life with her "Lion" aunt, getting no
farther than the exploration of words. I'm still
waving, not drowning. Dog and youth turn as
one and disappear into the green gloom of their
riverbank.

I swim back to the island, climb out onto fine
white river sand. Then I walk home up Main Street
drip drying in the heat. Hot people smirk. What are
they smirking at? Who suffers now?

At the end of Maple Street, the huge crane turns
on its tiny base. The parking lot is not finished
after all.

I went into labor at six in the morning. We were
in England at the time, stuck in a hotel somewhere
near Shepperton Studios because he was making a
picture. Even though I was virtually full term, he
couldn't resist the offer. Cream of British talent, he
said, from the director down to the best boy. Not
to mention going up against Anthony Hopkins. He
always needed to test himself against what he called
the "Big Boys." And I had to come along, all the way
from Malibu; he couldn't do it without me. What he
meant was, he was afraid he'd lose to a "Big Boy"
and then where would he hide? In me, of course.

In any case, of the two of us only I could give
birth, and only I could drive the rental car. So I

drove him to the hospital. But first I had to get him to a liquor store, which wasn't easy. Buying alcohol isn't the same in England as it is in Hollywood. But, believe you me, we succeeded. I may have been in ever increasing pain, but he was having a full blown head-on contrapuntal of a panic attack.

I also found the hospital after a lot of stopping and asking.

He arrived in maternity bearing a clanking canvas bag of some strong North Country brew, and I brought up the rear, bearing Kate. I spent the next thirty-six hours squeezing Kate out of me and into our unsuitable world, and he spent it coming and going and filming and drinking and becoming more and more British by the swallow. When Kate was finally hauled out into the cold chrome and colder white of an English delivery room, he took one look at her tiny gray body and howled, "Where's its bloody willy!"

He had Anthony Hopkins down pat.

I can write a thing—but can I do a thing?

"Midnight. Our hero enters the forbidden room, silently slipping in & out of shadows. He is wary, but determined."

No director, no camera, no script—just me standing on the edge of revelation. I've already discovered that what can be done in a heated frenzy of passion is not so easily accomplished in cold blood. Here I am, in the night, in the dark, a true intruder, a real sneak thief—and I am about to pee myself. It's not so much fear, as embarrassment. How foolish I'll feel getting booked down at the Little Sokoki cop shop.

With this thought, the fear of feeling foolish is

swiftly replaced by the terror of getting caught. I can't get caught.

But here I am anyway.

Gone two in the morning. I've waited until the last show at the River House Theater let out (my Malibu neighbor's latest comic book superhero flick had a short run; it's been replaced by something animated), until *The Last Ditch* emptied its patrons into the streets, until River House had settled into sleep. And then I waited a half hour more. In case "she" came walking and knocking at my door.

Now, I insert stolen key into the lock and turn. Door opens with a shriek. Didn't do that this morning. I freeze against the wall as the eternal seconds tick by. But no one opens another of the doors along the hall of the second floor.

What am I thinking? Why should they? We all live with the walking girl-woman. By now, it seems it would take Jacob Marley's ghost to attract their midnight attention.

Wary, determined, tongue stuck to the top of my mouth, I slip inside and lock the door.

It's pitch black in here. Benjamin Willow's drapes are drawn. I knew they would be. On the single day he spends "at work," Benjamin opens his drapes. On the days he is not here, they're closed. But I dare not turn on a light. Light might leak around the drapes. There might be someone out there, unable to sleep, and walking. The police might cruise by.

But I've planned for this. I've brought my Price Chopper flashlight. And my hammer.

The stairs behind my closet are real. I know they are. I've coughed their dust out of my lungs, been comforted by their light. Yet I can't find a trace of them on a single drawing. By flashlight, I've made my way to the remembered right hand wall, peered at the framed architectural designs of the 1867 River House for an hour now. Floor by floor. Room by room. From lobby to ballroom.

I've discovered that my third floor room was carved from a much larger room, was once rather nice. That Benjamin Willow's second floor office was once two rooms, and neither one as grand as mine once was. That the trendy dry goods store on the corner of Main and High, two floors below my room, and now just beneath my feet, was once a very grand hotel desk and, behind that, private offices. Best of all, Miss Jackson's office was once the linen supply closet. Being as petty as the next person, I like that.

But aside from the main stairs in the center of the building (which are still there), and aside from smaller emergency staircases on each end of the two wings (also still there), I can find no other stairs.

Even so, I've discovered how one gets into the tallest tower.

There is a sixth floor. Actually, it does not qualify as a floor. More like a cottage. A private cottage. On the roof of the Main Street wing of River House, and seen only as a curious ridge of extra roof from below, is a conceit, a folly, a very small one-story building sitting atop a very large five-story building. And in it was once a bijouterie of an apartment. Kitchen, two bedrooms, parlor, dining room, formal drawing room, office (called here a library), bath, separate toilet. There is a hallway running the length of the roof top apartment which divides the bedrooms, the library, and the large bath from the parlor, the drawing room, kitchen and dining room. At one end of this hallway is a tall window looking out over Main Street and what was once the large island in the middle of the Connecticut River. At the other end of this hallway there is a French door leading out onto the roof. From this roof, it is a short, and I'll bet, slightly dangerous walk to the central tower sitting like a single pawn on the edge of an empty chessboard. In the central tower there is a lower window that can't be seen from the street.

By Jove, as Sherlock would say, I have found it. This is the way into the tower.

Written in a pretty hand on the bottom of a drawing of the little house on the rooftop of River House, it says: *Private residence of Charles River Akeley & family.*

All this I have learned, but I still have no proof there are stairs in the back of my closet. One other thing: I haven't found the stairs up to the private home on the roof of River House either. But they must be around somewhere.

My nose is practically touching the glass of the fifth floor display, looking for those stairs, when I hear something at the door. A voice. Two voices. If I were nervous before, now I am preternatural with shock. I cannot leave by another door. There is no other door. I cannot hide in the closet. If there is a closet, I would have to find it in the dark—and very quickly. I can do nothing but duck down behind the shadowy bulk of Benjamin's desk. Which is not quite where I remembered it being. But near enough.

Snapping off my flashlight, I am down before a second second ticks by.

The door is more kicked open than pushed open. It slams back into the wall with a bang. By the sound of things, two bodies tumble out of the second floor hallway, laughing, bringing themselves and a splash of light into the darkened room. One is male and one is female and one of these two, I'm not sure which, is in a wheelchair. The male is slightly the worse for drink, that much is obvious. Mixed in with the heady scent of lilac comes the heady smell of whiskey. One of them gropes for a light and at the same time kicks the door closed. Door slams shut and light comes on simultaneously.

I am crouched down, not daring to peer out, not daring even to open my eyes. I'm as small as I can make myself behind the desk. And I hear this—

Female: "Stella's sure to scold me for letting you out tonight."

Male: "Forget about Stella, Lisa. I'm not telling if you're not telling."

(The audience and I now know the woman's name. It's Lisa. Though Stella remains a mystery.)

Male: "Wheel me up to the window. Right here will do just fine. Say! You see that!"

Lisa: "See what?"

Male: "You want to hand me that camera, the one with the telephoto lens?"

Lisa (almost laughing, but not really): "No."

Male (actually laughing): "Don't be like that. I'm only getting to know the neighbors. Be a good girl, pass me my camera."

Lisa must have done just that from the sounds I hear, because now comes the snap of a case opening, of a wheelchair's brake being locked. "I'm turning off the light, Lisa. You better move over there."

The light goes out. Comes on again.

Lisa: "I'm afraid of the dark. I like the light on."

Light goes out.

Male (his voice lower): "You want them all to see us?"

Lisa (a little shrill now): "Stop it, Jeff. Someone's bound to see you. You'll get reported. What will you say? I was only keeping an eye on them? Like any good neighbor would do."

(And now we know his name. It's Jeff.)

"Well, yes. That's exactly what I'll say. Of course, if you'd just leave the lights alone, I wouldn't have to say any such thing."

Light on. Light off. Something crashes onto the floor. A book? A paperweight? A shoe? A hammer?

Lisa: "All right. Have it your way. I think I'll go now. Jeff, did you hear me? I said I'm leaving."

Lisa must be closer to me than Jeff is. I can hear her breathing. I know how she's feeling. She feels as I used to feel when he ignored me, made me disappear in his mind. It hurts terribly. So she's doing what I seldom did. She really is leaving. I listen as she works her way to the door in the dark, then opens it. Pale light leaks in from the hall.

Jeff: "Shut the door, Lisa. It's too bright."

Lisa is gone.

But I'm not. I'm hiding behind a couch and the way things look, I'll be hiding behind a couch for a long time. Hold on. I should be behind Benjamin's desk, not a couch. This can't be right. I unravel from my position, flashlight in one hand, hammer in the other, at the same time moving round the couch/desk.

Jeff: "You can come out now."

What? Is he speaking to me? Or Lisa? I can't open my mouth. If I could, no word would come out of it. My tongue is sunken, dry as river sand. I can't turn on the flashlight. I can't stand up.

Suddenly, the light goes on.

I'm not behind Benjamin's desk. Or even behind a couch. I'm standing in the middle of the room. Alone.

Is it worse to discover there is no one here with me, in a wheelchair or not in a wheelchair, or—is it worse to find that it is not Benjamin's office? Have I broken and entered the wrong room? Of course I haven't entered the wrong room. What about the architectural drawings I've just been studying?

I turn. The drawings are not there. Instead, I find myself in a room that is twice the size of Benjamin Willow's office. It's furnished like a suite, a tasteful hotel suite that you'd see in a movie made in the late Thirties when the Hays Code was in its prime. Two single beds, a black phone in an upright cradle on the nightstand between them, an art deco vanity. The mirror over the vanity, shaped like the top of the Chrysler Building, shows me... *me.* I'm dressed like Carole Lombard in a screwball comedy. Only lately a mess, my hair is marcelled.

If I knew how to faint, I would faint. All I know how to do is close my eyes and hold on to what is left of my mind. When I open my eyes again, it will be Benjamin Willow's office and in one of Benjamin's windows Jimmy Stewart, another dead movie star, will be a middle-aged man in a wheelchair looking out through the old and wavy glass through a telephoto lens. Or he'll be looking at me. Either way, Jimmy playing Jeff will be here.

I open my eyes. There is no one here. But me. No mirror, but I can see my own shaking flashlight in my own shaking hand.

I'm in Benjamin's office. I throw up in Benjamin's private toilet.

And now, here I am, trying to sit very still on Benjamin's office chair—and I breathe. In. Out. In. Out. In. Holding on to my breath in the hopes of holding on to my sanity. That is, if I am still sane. Or ever was. Was I? Was he? Is anyone? How can we be if Shirley is right and reality, absolute or otherwise, is not?

My story is not going to end well. I knew that before I came here. But to become a Hitchcock of a story? I hadn't intended that at all.

Alfred once stayed here. In River House. He was making a movie and while he was making his movie, he lived in one of these rooms, worked out his stories in one of these rooms. Are his stories still here? Is that how strong story is? Can dreams imbed themselves in the walls? Can they come out and play in the mind...in the right mind? One like mine, for instance. One possessed by a tale of pity and woe. Lovecraft also once stayed here. Hitchcock now playing in the Theater of the Mind is one thing. Lovecraft is another thing altogether.

Has it come to this? Are we insane, my imagination and I?

He used to say imagination was a curse. He used to say there was nothing that was not imagined. He once said we are all trapped in story.

But when you lose a child, you lose all the stories you have ever lived, all you had hoped to live, and there is only one story left—tragic and final.

Others have cracked up for less. Our daughter is dead. He is dead. My work is dead. I am dead. Or soon will be.

For a dead woman, I'm horribly scared—unsettled beyond anything I have ever described in book or script as unsettled. No screaming though. No running in circles. Just a nice straight drop into real trouble. Like missing a step, not on stairs, but at the edge of a cliff.

What do I do now? What would Hitchcock do? I'm not the slightest interested in what Lovecraft would do.

I've been in my room for three days, not leaving it for any reason. No pretence at writing, I lie here on the floor and watch the shadows come and go on my walls. I pee. I shit. Though of course, without eating, this happens less and less. Even the hunger grows less. I do drink. But city tap water, not booze. All the booze is down the drain and into the river. Late at night I listen to the woman who walks the halls. Each night, she stops at my door but she has not knocked. It wouldn't matter if she did. I would not answer. I tell myself to relax. I do not scream. I endure strange states, strange sensations, morbid fantasies. I do not look in the closet.

There are some things even I do not deserve. On the fourth day, I shower.

Is it safe to go out now?

The mind is a resilient thing. The will to survive indomitable. I've half convinced myself that the scene in Benjamin Willow's office, which was not Benjamin Willow's office, was the television in a nearby apartment and that someone was watching *Rear Window*. I imagine that for a moment something freakish happened to the sound waves: they got louder, much louder, even rewriting a whole scene. Science is not my strong suit. As far as I know, things like that happen, like getting Radio Free Europe through old fashioned dental fillings. Or. It did not happen. It was an aural hallucination brought on by nerves. And if the off-the-cuff adventure of Jeff and Lisa was a private, very personal, movie made by me for the audience of myself, then perhaps other things are also little movies played on the screen of my tormented psyche. The figures glimpsed briefly in windows. The stairs in the back of my closet. Even, perhaps, the woman, once old and now not old at all, who cannot keep still, the one Miss Jackson says does not live in River House.

I have a right to be nervous. I have a reason to be frightened. There are Los Angeles cops on my tail—perhaps by now even federal cops. After all, I've crossed a lot of state lines. I've crossed a lot of lines. Surely, they must have some idea of where I am. They found him weeks ago. Isn't the spouse the first person suspected? Especially a missing spouse?

No matter. I must eat. I ran out of seeds some time back. Can't remember when. But it's not time to die yet.

A bell peals out from one of the churches on Main Street. Little Sokoki is full of churches, most of them white in both paint and congregation. After that comes more and more and more until the air is full of an irritating bing bong clanging. Is it Sunday?

The man who will give Faye away, Mr. Hunnicutt from the white Colonial next door to Faye's little brown saltbox, smiles at her from his place on the aisle. Mr. Hunnicutt knows what to wear to a wedding. A nice black suit with a soft white shirt and bright yellow tie. Mr. Hunnicutt is nearsighted. He doesn't notice when Faye does not smile back. There is no best man because as a traveler, Mr. Honig has no friends in Wobanaki Falls. There are no bride's maids or flower girls because it has not occurred to Faye to ask anyone. There is a pastor. He is the very tall man waiting near the organ. Pastor Bruce is scandalized by the bride's dress. But too civilized to say so.

Where is Mr. Honig?

What would Faye do if she even suspected Mr. Honig had run away?

No finding out because here he is now. He's slipped in quietly and is standing by Pastor Bruce at the front of the church. Mr. Honig is dressed as any respectable groom should be dressed. He even has a flower in his buttonhole. Yellow. Is it a carnation? Or a mum? His tie is yellow as well. Truth to tell, there are many among the guests who are quite disappointed in Mr. Honig. To compete with the red dress, some feel the least he

could have done is worn golf shoes and a
Tyrolean hat. But Mr. Honig's appearance
goes a long way to mollifying the pastor. He
is the most unexceptional looking man Pastor
Bruce has ever seen.

As for Faye, she's also quite satisfied.
She grips Mr. Hunnicutt's offered arm as the
organist begins to play the Wedding March.

And so they are wed. Faye, handsome as
a horse and determined as an ant, becomes
Mrs. Honig without further ado. Mrs. Honig
in her red red dress, Mr. Honig in his yellow
rose (up close, it's a rose) and yellow tie. The
wedding guests, their disappointment in the
groom forgotten minutes into the ceremony,
sniffle among themselves as good wedding
guests always do.

It's over. The wedding party spills
out onto the sidewalk in front of the white
church...and for just a moment the bells that
peal out from the slender white steeple sound
like real bells.

I almost faint on my way to Price Chopper.

Confused by specks and bars and zigzags of
broken light, I tremble as I walk, weave across the
sidewalk, come close to feeling my way. The hell
with this. I am not dying by starvation, and I'm
fucked if I'm cracking open my head on cement.

Vachel Lindsay drank Lysol. Sara Teasdale, the
poet he loved all his life, was much kinder to herself
than that. She took sleeping pills, slowly dying in
a warm bath. Richard Brautigan shot himself, but
left a great suicide note. It said, "Messy, isn't it?"

Hemingway, who had no sense of humor, at least
not about himself, seated his manly ass near the
entrance of his house so no one could miss him,
and then took his entire head off with a shotgun
blast. Now, *that* was messy. John Kennedy Toole,
when he couldn't get published for love or money,
stuck a garden hose on the exhaust pipe of his car.
Sylvia Plath stuck her head in an oven. Even the
Singing Nun and her female lover, both voluntarily
unfrocked and together to the end, washed down
massive doses of barbiturates with alcohol. All
effective ways to go, but not my way. Especially
Lindsay and his Lysol. That must have taken some
nerve. That had to be the very last word in a big
"Fuck You, World." As for Plath, the patron saint
of schoolgirl angst—when Sylvia did herself in, her
two kids were at home. With her. In the house
with her. She made them cookies. She gave each
a glass of milk. She waited until they were asleep
in their rooms. Be that as it may, her two small
children, as absorbent as sponges in the sea, were
there to find their mommy gassed in the oven that
baked their cookies. She might as well have killed
them too. She did kill them, or some part of them.
I hate Sylvia Plath.

I'm going to eat something; I'm regaining my
strength. By now I know I won't be writing a last
book, but perhaps I can manage one more film
script. If I can hallucinate a riff on someone else's
movie, I should be able to manage one of my own.

I devour a tuna melt from the deli section,
ignore the stares (startled, sullen, suspicious, do I
look that bad?) of my fellow Little Sokoki shoppers,
am about to walk back to River House with a bag
of bagels and a block of cream cheese, when I find

I'm standing in front of the wines. One bottle of something light and fruity is civilized. It's good for the heart. It goes well with cheese. I will buy only one.

I buy three. Heavy. Red. French. Who knows when I'll get back to the store now I'm writing a screenplay? I already know just the person to play me. Granted, she's putting on some age; even so, she's still box office. She'll think it's the role of a lifetime. She'll snatch it away before my agent can finish his pitch. Especially if I change things a little, make myself younger, prettier, more successful: tougher, thinner, scarier. And it won't make a fuckwad of difference to either of them if I'm a convicted murderer. Actually, in Hollywood, a murderer's price goes up.

INTERIOR. NIGHT.

I've been writing for hours. Night presses its bony spine against my window. And the words spill out of me. I am fertile. I am working. I am alive. I am drinking but I scarcely feel it save for the lift in my blood.

I could not be insane. Not with such a perfect set-up, such telling touches of character. No one who's lost it could write with such clarity. I almost wonder if I will have to change the ending. I refer to my own. There are, after all, only three kinds of endings. Happy, sad, and ironic. My original ending was sad. I'm talking metaphorically here. And I'm not fool enough to think it will ever be happy. But now I lean towards the ironic. Could my guilty heroine live to fight another day? I don't know yet. I'll let the movie tell me.

There is a knock on my door, and I am suddenly a landed fish with the shock of it, flopping on my futon. My laptop skitters off my stomach and onto the carpet.

What? What! Oh for god's sake. Not now. Go away. You're not real. I'm working here.

It comes again. Louder.

This time I shout: "Bugger off!"

But the knocking continues, more insistent. Blam! Blam! Blam!

I can't bloody believe it. Just when I'm coming to a crucial bit, a section of dialogue I must get just right—and I almost had it, I could almost hear it, but now it's lost in the shock of the knocking at my door.

That's it. That caps it. Real or not real, who does she think she is, pounding on my door? Who does she think I am? Well, little darlin', you're about to find out. What I did once, I can do again.

I am up off the floor and across the room lickety-split. Grabbing the doorknob, I yank open my door. No one there, but I'm ready for this. In men's pajama bottoms and a tee shirt, I'm out in the hall on the instant, fast enough to see something flit round the corner at the end of the third floor corridor. She's quick, no doubt about it, but not quick enough. I saw her. Not clearly, but clearly enough to know she's on the stairs at the end of the High Street wing of River House.

Barefoot, I streak for the emergency staircase. Of course she's already gone by the time I reach the head of the stairs. Has she gone down? Or up? I wait for a moment, straining to hear.

Down.

I leap down, two steps at a time. It's late. If

91

someone hears us—two people running pell-mell down the stairs in the middle of the night—fuck 'em.

The emergency fire door is swinging shut on the second floor landing. She's not leaving the building so she must live on the second floor. Or she must know someone who lives on the second floor. I have her. If I have to knock on every door on the second floor, I damn well will. I know what I am capable of. Knocking on doors in River House in the middle of the night pales by comparison.

She couldn't have reached the turn at the end of the corridor. This section is half a block long. Not enough time. I imagine her crouched inside one of the doors on the High Street wing, her ear pressed hard against it, listening for me. She knows where I am. Where else would I be? Does she imagine herself safe? I imagine she does.

But this is my movie now.

It used to be his movie. It was his needs we tended to, his talent we made room for, his dream we followed, his demons tormenting us. For the longest time, I questioned none of this. Of course he came first. He was a genius. He was a Golden Globe, Spirit Award, Bafta Awards, Oscar winning movie star.

We met on the set of *The Windigo's Daughter*. I was there as the writer. Lowly writers aren't usually allowed within a mile of a movie set, but this day was the director's idea of an "open house." He was there because he had a small, but exceedingly crucial, part. It was my idea to get him to play it: after all, I wrote it for him. Somebody must have told him that, because during a break he came looking for me. Bold as chili. Sober as water. Nothing coy, nothing worked out beforehand, just a straight forward try for a quick fuck. If he were here now, he'd tell you different, but he didn't get laid the day we met. The day we met we sat and talked in canvas chairs provided by whoever provides canvas chairs on movie sets (mine said "Visitor;" his said "Mr. Nelson" which meant it was the director's chair), and then in his dressing room because we were pissing off the director by making him stand. And then, when the set shut down late in the day, we talked all the way to my Topanga Canyon rental where I picked up something to swim in (cut-offs and a tank top), and then all the way to his place in Malibu where we got towels so we could lie on the narrow beach in front of his house and watch the sun go down over Santa Catalina and the fog roll in. We talked through every moment of all this. He made me cry because he scared me. I thought I'd found a mentor, someone to help me grow up. I thought he saw me. I thought he saw through me. It scared me half to death to be seen, but I couldn't stop myself letting him look. He got laid the day after we met: on the pebbled beach, near the deep sea stink of the pilings under his beach house. It was cold and sticky and exposed and stupid so we went inside, showered off, and did it again in his nice big unmade bed overlooking the hissing sea. Much better.

Innocent me. I knew he drank. But I had this truly naive idea that talking as we had talked and fucking as we fucked would give him reason to stop drinking. Or, second best, slow it down a little.

None of the doors on either side of the High

93

Street second floor hall are open. They wouldn't be. She had time to close a door.

I creep along in the eternal light—the halls of River House are kept lit all day and all night. Dim light, yet I see everything: the stains on the worn brown carpet, the dull gleam on the dun painted walls, the scuffs on the dark brown doors—kicks? drunken falls? Overhead the ceilings are lowered just as they are in the rooms. Thin yellowed tiles. Exposed sprinkler systems. An exit sign far away at the turn of the hall.

It's as if River House quietly breathes. Like an old man breathes, lying in bed, covers up to his chin, waiting.

Shall I knock on the first door I come to—or the last?

I choose the first door. I square up to it, preparing myself for what is bound to come when you knock on a door in the dead of night. Head up, eyes steady in their sockets, words steady in my throat, my arm raised, my knuckles ready—but just as they begin their descent, I hear something. It's behind me. So faint a noise, it seems nothing more than a change in air pressure, but I hear it, and I turn. A door has opened along the hall. A door that was firmly shut a moment ago is now open a crack.

Determined, I begin my stride towards it. And then suddenly stop. It's the door to Benjamin Willow's office.

Back in my room again. I could not go there. I cannot go there. Did she know that? She knew that.

In a horror movie, someone always plays the

one person who hears something in a haunted house—and walks towards it. This someone— usually young, usually female, usually half- dressed—is called the "idiot-in-the-attic." She climbs the blood drenched stairs up into the creaking attic, or down into the moaning pitch- black cellar, or opens the door to the closet. And all the while the audience, knowing better, pleads with her: Stop! Get out of there, you moron. Run for your life!

I'm not an idiot-in-the-attic. But I might be an idiot.

If I were fully alive, I'd leave. Right now. In the middle of the night. If I weren't who I am, hadn't done what I've done, I wouldn't spend another night here. All those years ago, I was right. There's something wrong with River House. Somewhere inside it there's a world of lunatic darkness that no longer allures. It no longer seems enchanted. It's not a palace. It's a madhouse. I am sick with fear.

I was braver at twelve than I am at my eternal thirty-six. This isn't what I planned.

Here I am, in my room, and I laugh. I lean against my feature wall and I laugh and laugh. I've seen all this in movies. The laughing lunatic scene. And what do you know...lunatics do laugh. Lunatics laugh until they throw up. If there is nothing wrong with River House, then there is certainly something wrong with me. Hell. Of course there's something wrong with me. There is something very wrong with me. There are some things you do in a life that you cannot undo. There are some things that are unforgivable. Aside from that, I'm suicidal. I'm sure that qualifies as a problem.

What would a therapist say?

In Malibu, he had a therapist. As a healer, his therapist was useless. As a drug dispenser, she was invaluable. I could use one of her prescriptions now. Or an exorcist.

An exorcist?

I'm at my closet door, flinging it open, dragging out the locked leather bag. Large but not that heavy, it comes away easily, so easily that I stagger with it, fall on my ass. If the woman who walks the halls and hides in rooms isn't driving this building batty, I certainly am. Whoever lives beneath me must have heard that. What the hell.

Back up again, trying to open the bag. Christ, I remember. I locked it after I removed the hammer. I wasn't quite as crazy then. I still knew enough to lock things. And then I put the key somewhere safe. But where? In a frenzy now, I stand, spin where I stand. There's so few hiding places. It must be obvious. Why can't I remember?

There is a single knock at my door—and at the same moment the light comes on in the back of my closet. I've already forgotten what I hoped to find in my bag.

When I came home that day, he was asleep. Not a nap, or a snooze, but a coma...deep deep into the reeking pit of a drunk's complete oblivion. He was sprawled on the floor of her room, lying on her toys, on her scattered bedding. On the remains of her lunch. Her tiny spoon was still in his hand, creamed corn congealing on the soft tufted carpet. And Kate wasn't anywhere. She wasn't anywhere. I ran through the rooms, calling her name. And when she wasn't in the house, I ran outside. We lived in Malibu, but had no pool. She couldn't be in the pool. But she could be in the road, over a cliff, in a sack on the back of a madman.

"Katy! Katherine! Kate!"

By then I was screaming, my throat already shredded with the power of my shrieks.

I found her. We had no pool yet she had drowned anyway. Beyond an oleander hedge our next door neighbors had a pond. A large pond filled with goldfish. Untended, uncared for, unwatched, Kate must have tumbled in looking at the fish.

Our neighbor found me cradling Kate. I have no idea how long I had held her, talking, urging her home, willing her back into her small cold body.

She never came back. And neither have I.

The light is on again. It becomes obvious. If I am not insane, and even now I might not be, then I am being called. Something wants me to climb the stairs. If there are no stairs, if there never were any stairs, there are stairs now. Maybe they're my stairs. Maybe they show themselves only to me. One thing's for certain—I can see them as clearly as I can see my bare feet, dark gray on the bottom from running on the filthy carpets of River House.

But what, in anyone's life, is "real"? How much of what is yours is shared with others? We each see through our own unique eyes, feel with our own isolated hearts, perhaps we create our own personal reality by our own personal thoughts, our feelings? Perhaps everyone's an artist. Perhaps the whole world is a movie, and we are all screenwriters. Perhaps I created the stairs.

If I screamed, would they go away? If I climbed them, would I go away?

Sentences form in my mind. They are not whispered. They are not quietly declarative. They are a shout from the inside.

"You have nothing to lose. You have already lost it all. You're still a writer. Follow the story."

I climb the stairs. Which are not circular, not lit at the top, not filled with the music of Cole Porter. These stairs are very old and very bare. They are silent and narrow, wedged between the inner and outer walls of River House, and barely wide enough for my shoulders, barely lit enough to see each worn stair as I climb it. These stairs smell of mold.

Over the years I have had the same dream. Or versions of the same dream. I dream about a house. It ought to be my house, but it isn't. Someone has somehow taken it from me, changed it, made some rooms cozy, some strange. Put some in very out of the way places, left other rooms to rot. No matter how the house looks, I always know it is the same house and I wander around in it, never wondering at how big it is inside, how complex, when outside it seems so small. No matter how many stairs I climb, there is always another, higher, floor. No matter how deep I go into the cellar, there is always a deeper cellar.

I sob in my dreams. Whoever owns it or lives in it does not want me there. I am always the outsider sneaking around in someone else's house. It was my house once, and now I am an intruder in it. I am lost in it.

When I awake from one of my house dreams, I often think of Shirley Jackson who must have had similar dreams. In her house, whatever walked

there walked alone. In my house, I have company. In my house, and years and years before Kate drowned, I've looked for a lost child.

I think I am that child.

I don't know what I'm looking for now as I climb the stairs that lead up, and down, behind my closet. I don't know why I'm doing this. I thought I had something to do. Before it was too late to make choices, I would come to River House, I would write something, anything, one last time. I would see where that led me. I thought it was obvious. It would lead me to my final fatal "fini." It would be my big fadeout.

Now? Now, I don't know what the hell I'm doing.

I've lost track of time. I could have been climbing these stairs for five minutes. I could have been climbing them for five hours. Looking back down at the stairs I've climbed, they seem endless. Looking up towards those I've yet to climb, these also seem endless. No doors have led off from the odd little landings I've come to, narrow and without purpose, no windows have looked out at anything, or in at anything. The walls of the staircase are bare of paper, almost even of plaster. In many places the ancient lathe shows through. I can scarcely breathe for the dust, as thick as chaff. Glancing down at my pajama bottoms, I see they're coated with powdery debris. My feet are almost black, my hands gray.

It all smells of darkness, yet there is light. Not bright. Not coming from anywhere in particular. Maybe there is no light. Maybe I can see merely because I can *see*.

I ought to be still terrified, but I'm not. I'm numb. Not only have I lost track of time, but of purpose. Why am I climbing these stairs? What was I doing before I started climbing these stairs?

I can't remember. It seems I really am the ultimate idiot in the attic.

Fade to black.

I can almost count on it by now. I'm back in bed. I'm lying in my bed on the floor in my room in River House—no, wait, it's not on the floor. It's a proper bed, a double four-poster bed. Bit saggy, just the tiniest bit shabby, but it has decent sheets, a rather charming counterpane, and there's a nice little nightstand next to it. Oh look, a little handmade doily. I haven't seen one of those since Wichita. Mother covered everything in doilies, especially the top of her fucking piano. There's the book I brought with me. I went to sleep reading *Forever Amber*, by some fellow female named Kathleen Winsor. Seems appropriate. The heroine, Amber (and what kind of name is that?), sleeps her way higher and higher in the world. Wish I'd learned to do that. I've slept my way lower and lower. And there's the bottle of pills. Sometime today I'll take them. And then I'll see if I can finish *Forever Amber* before the barbiturates finish me.

Hah. I'm really a hoot today.

The phone on the nightstand rings. I won't answer it. I don't want to answer it. If I answer it, it'll be someone I don't want to speak to. It's never anyone I want to speak to.

I took a frigging bus all the way from New York City to get away from the phone, from the never-ending city bustle and heave, from the same

questions I've been asked now for years, from my
own stupid pointless mortality, and where does it
get me? The phone that's ringing keeps ringing
until it stops ringing. As soon as that happens, I
pick up the hand receiver, dial 0 for the desk.

"This is room 36. Yes, that's right, it's me, the
one who used to be a famous actress. Don't put
any more calls through, please. I don't care. Tell
them I'm sleeping. Tell them I've gone out. No,
better yet. Tell them I'm dead. Yes, even calls from
New York. No calls at all, you understand. Thank
you."

That crack about telling 'em I'm dead...no one
takes you seriously when you say things like that.
And thank heavens they don't, or I'd have half
this town in my room. Fucking Hollywood press.
They've killed more than me in their time.

Bless bloody Greta. She knew when to get
out. And so did I. Trouble with me and not with
Greta, is I didn't know enough not to come back.
But here's a true blue fact: Greta would have
backstroked through mud if those fat boorish buck-
on-the bottom-line Jewish boobs had asked her
real nice. And stopped with the lesbian smut. So
she liked muff? So do I. Enough, anyway, for an
evening's amusement. So fucking what?

I've got two packages of Chesterfields on the
dresser and a fifth of Gordon's gin in a drawer in
the big wardrobe by the door to the bathroom. I've
got all I need, don't have to go out for anything. I
can't stand going out. Every time I go out, it's
always the same. Samuel L. Christ, I haven't
made a moving picture for years, and there's still
someone who stops me on the street.

What the hell is the terrible row outside the

102

window? You'd think this was Paris the day the Germans showed up, not some nothing little town in Vermont.

I go to the window. It's not Paris. The German army isn't out there. It's just Vermont where a couple of working joes are busy dismantling a perfectly splendid iron balcony one floor down from my window. No doubt it's getting turned over to the government as scrap metal so the government can beat it into tanks. As Tallulah would say, "Too fabulous." I do wish someone had told me they were doing this before I checked in last night. I could have found somewhere else to drop dead in.

Oh for God's sake, now what? Someone's knocking on the door. I'll have to answer. I can't sulk in here forever like some people I can think of. Plus, I'm not dead yet.

On the third knock, I yank open the door. Not quite what I expected, but bad enough.

"Miss Brooks?"

"Yes."

The woman is trembling. She's clutching her little menu, crushing it, she's so thrilled it's me, really me. Poor silly foolish thing.

"Management asked me to tell you if you wanted anything, anything at all, please don't hesitate to ask. I mean, it's you. You're her."

"So I am."

She thrusts the menu at me, but I'm already shutting the door. If I don't she'll be weeping soon, and I'll have to invite her in, and then she'll tell me I'm her favorite movie star and why oh why don't I make any more pictures?

As I'm sliding the little whatsit that dead bolts the door, and catching sight of the bottle of pills on my nightstand, I give the woman an unspoken answer to her unasked question. Because they don't want me, that's why, girlie. They don't want me in their movies. They don't want me on their radio shows. They don't even want me behind their counters in Saks fucking Fifth Avenue. But I'll show the bastards.

Pad over and get the gin out of the wardrobe drawer, pad back to the four-poster. Don't need a glass. Straight out of the bottle will do. Set that down on my nightstand. Pick up the pills, shake a few into my hand. How many are lethal? Who knows? Who cares? I'll take 'em all. But not yet. Like to enjoy a drink or two, a few more chapters of my book. I'll take two pills, see how that feels, and then take the rest when I'm feeling really calm and sleepy. What could be easier?

I've got all day to die. Why rush it?

So here I am in some big old hotel in little old Vermont with birds on the wallpaper, birds and vines and flowers, and I'm reading *Forever Amber*. It's only just come out, and bingo, already whoever this Winsor dame is, she's rich and famous. Now that's a field I should have gone into, rather than dancing since I was a little kid. And especially rather than acting. Stupid thing to do, act. Always felt like a damn fool. Plus writers don't get told they're too old to write, or that nobody wants to see their sorry face on a giant screen anymore. Writers just write. And they don't kill themselves.

You know, this is a great book. I'm supposed to be dying here, and I can't put down the book. Wish I could write something people couldn't put down. Say, what a joke that would be. What a laugh. If I wrote something that sold like this. Or even if I just wrote something that'd make their Hollywood hair stand on end. Inside stuff. The straight dope.

I sit up straighter. Pills are making me slump here a little. But Jesus, I really could do it. Not a novel, not right out of the gate, but a tell-all kind of thing. *Lulu in Hollywood* by Louise Brooks. It'd sell like peaches.

For the first time in years I feel almost light-hearted. It won't last, it never does. Besides, it's probably the pills. And the shot of gin I chased 'em down with. But really, thinking about it, if I die, they win. But if I learn to become a writer, why heck, they lose.

I can dance. I can act. I can talk. I can do all sorts of things. How hard can it be to write?

Quick as quick, I've flushed the rest of the pills down the toilet. Half the bottle too, though I keep the other half. No use wasting good liquor. I have a book to read. A skill to learn. And a whole day to lie in bed doing it.

Outside my window they're beating beautiful old balconies into guns. No one's doing that to me. Boy, will I show 'em.

I wake up screaming, a scream cut off before it gets out of my mouth, as well as out of hand. That was a dream. Was that a dream? It wasn't a dream. I have no dreams, except my house dreams. I don't know what it was. I don't know who I am.

The taste in my mouth, it's like everyone says, an ashtray. I don't smoke. I've never smoked. My whole room reeks of cigarette smoke.

Did I get up the stairs? Was I climbing the stairs?

I'm lying on my bed on the floor with what remains of the thin dirty-yellow ceiling tiles above my head and the sun through my window squatting on my chest like a golden toad. That, and my laptop. Which begins to seem more than toadish. It begins to seem an incubus.

Can't help it. My eyes drop to the screen. What now? Well, of course, my screenplay is gone.

I can't breathe. I hurt. I hurt everywhere.

Must pee. Must pee so bad I can feel it in my teeth. My teeth are vibrating. Crawl off my bed, crawl across the floor, moaning with pain. Closet door is closed. I whine deep in my throat as I crawl past it. There are no stairs in the back of my closet. No Hitchcock movie playing in Benjamin's office which isn't Benjamin's office. No scaly woman who walks the halls of River House knocking on doors, on my door. I'm not Louise Brooks hiding in River House when it was still River House, come to kill myself with barbiturates and a bottle of Gordon's Gin. There is only me and I'm done for. There's only moonstruck me. I'm round the twist. I'm off the deep end. I blew my mind out in a car in a bar in a moment of divine apoplectic rage. I'm wiggy, bonkers, and bonzo. And worst of all, no matter how I suffer, I'm still a mid-list fair-to-middling writer.

When the police finally catch up with me, and they will catch up with me, I'll be a liquefying mess in the corner.

I sit on the toilet and pee. My pee feels high octane, 180 proof. I must have a fever. Do I have a fever? Do I have a thermometer in order to know if I have a fever?

Would crying help?

I'm finished. I'm packed. I'm leaving. I have
the door open, am almost out in the hall when I
notice I'm not dressed. I'm still in my tee shirt
and his pajama bottoms, dirty from the stairs. I'm
barefooted. Does it matter? It matters. Being
crazy is bad enough. Looking crazy will get you
netted.

Of course, if I'm really crazy, how do I hide
from myself? This is a strangely encouraging
thought. Seriously crazy people have already
hidden from themselves by being seriously crazy.
Seriously crazy people don't know they're crazy.
The world is full of people: religious zealots,
religious fundamentalists, radicals, terrorists,
serial killers, housewives, husbands hiding in front
of TV screens, teenagers, corporate drones, stock
brokers, CEOs, high ranking military personnel,
politicians, directors, producers, judges, members
of the Federal Reserve, major writers and major
movie stars, and every one of them unaware they're
insane.

Pulling on jeans over his pajamas, a sweater
over my tee shirt, song lyrics sound in my head:
You can run, but you can't hide. I think: No, but I
can run and run and run and run and maybe then
I'll be too busy to worry about whether I'm nuts or
not. Isn't that what running is for? Also shopping,
shooting up, belting down, seeking public office,
making one more bet, and screwing strangers?
Anything that takes you past the pain of looking at
yourself.

I'll get dressed. And then I'll get very busy
running.

I wake up and the first thing I see, inches from my face, is a blank white Word Doc. The curser pulses at the far left. There's nothing on the page. Nothing. Is it my laptop? Is this a new twist? The Haunted Laptop. Should I call my agent—pitch it as a horror movie for yuppies?

I don't understand. Don't understand. Don't. Dreaming. I must have been dreaming. Must get a grip.

Moving only my head, I turn slowly towards the door. My big leather bag is packed, which means I must have found the key. When did I do that? Where was it? Why did I want it before? My laptop case is beside it. I look down the length of my body. I'm wearing jeans and a sweater. I'm even wearing shoes.

So it's true. It happened. I tried to leave.

If I tried to leave, why aren't I gone?

Smiling fondly, Mr. Honig holds out his hand to Mrs. Honig, who makes a snatch for the hand, gets a good hold, and propels him back along Cherry Street, followed by the wedding guests. From Cherry, they careen left into West Hackmatack Street, followed by the wedding guests. Faye's street is a golden vault roofed with turning leaves. As they hurry along, everyone kicks up the crackling leaves of maple and oak, of butternut and birch, of ash and apple and beech.

At her own gate, Mrs. Honig pauses... which gives Mr. Honig and the wedding guests time to catch their breath.

All is well, thinks Faye. The Wobanaki

Falls's catering van is parked out front. Which
means, of course, the wedding feast has
arrived. Left to herself, there would be no
wedding feast. No feast, that is, for anyone
other than Mrs. Honig...but only if she's
naughty—and my, how she'd regret that in the
morning. The reception has been Mr. Honig's
idea. As a traveling man, he'd said, with his
only home a room in a hotel, he kind of had
his heart set on a real reception in a tent on
her back lawn. But for the time it used up,
Faye couldn't see the harm in it. The reception
is why there are any wedding guests in the
first place. Mr. Honig had gone round asking
each and every one of them only these past
few days. A woman of no subtlety, Faye
never wonders why everyone came.

   Mr. Honig reaches past Mrs. Honig to open
the gate for her and to hold it open.

   He never left me, but I left him. I was bloated
with baby; he was sprawled on the back deck
snoring off his latest drunken funfest with his latest
set of drunken funfest friends, actors all. Some
were famous, some were famous and women. Two
were girls, starlets, poor starry eyed fools. But
most were males. My house smelled like beer and
bourbon, sweat and vomit. It also smelled like
dope. And sex. The "friends" were still draped
around the deck and my living room waiting to
wake up and start it all over again. I should have
taken photographs, sold them to the tabloids,
used the money for my baby and me. Instead, I
drove myself to Tombstone, Arizona. Who goes

to Tombstone, Arizona in August? No one sane.
Which is why I went—no one would look for me
there. I managed a week before he found me.
For some reason, waking up to discover me gone
sobered him up. He threw every last "friend" out
of the house, hired a cleaning service who virtually
hosed the place down, at the same time hiring a
detective who detected me in about four hours flat
(which is why I know about credit cards and why
this time they're cut into tiny pieces and buried
under a rock near Alice's defunct Restaurant, and
why I don't use my actual name, or call or write
anyone, or allow my photo to be taken). When I
answered the phone in my Tombstone motel room
he made one of his promises. It was soulfully done.
I think he meant it. But then, he always meant it.
I came home from Arizona.

I'd give anything if I hadn't. I'd give anything
to be walking past the OK Corral right this minute,
in a pair of old jeans with the knees busted out, a
month's rent in the bank, holding down a job at the
Doc Holiday Convenience Store, and leading Kate
on her pony. We should have bought a pony. I
should have bought a horse. We should have called
her pony Wyatt. Bullets couldn't touch Wyatt Earp.

Yet again, there's nothing to eat. I've looked
three times and each time there is the same
nothing in the refrigerator, the same nothing in
the dark brown cabinets over the tin sink. There's
nothing to drink except tap water.

I think I'll lie down now and wait. For a pizza
delivery, for the dark, for the end. Whichever
comes first.

Knock on the door.

Pizza?

Swaying with dizziness, gathering myself to face what must be faced, I lurch to the door and yank it open. It's the young man with the camcorder. Not that he has a camcorder now. He has an apple.

He holds out the apple, blood red and tempting. Or it would be if I could eat an apple on an empty stomach. He says, "Are you okay?"

I stare at him. Am I okay? No. I am not okay. I have never been okay. I'm freaking and stinking in a doorway in River House, and nothing has ever been okay. I want to tell him I have never been smart enough, pretty enough, thin enough, talented enough, ambitious enough. All I've ever done is practice enough. I've written for years, published for years. And after all these years, all these words? I am not fucking good enough. My work isn't good enough. I'm missing something. Depth? Heart? Intelligence? Raw talent? The right idea at the right time?

Somerset Maugham would say he was the best of the second raters. I can't even aspire to that.

Most of all, I haven't been loved enough. Not by him. Not by me. Poor me.

And then there's Kate. Poor Kate. And then there's the little matter of the mess I made in Malibu.

Knowing how I must look, how I must smell, I work up a little smile. Close to the bottom, I'm still political, still feminine, still hoping to please to keep from being hit, hurt, rejected. I say, "Of course I'm okay. Thank you for asking."

I close the door on his smile. I close the door on his apple. One way or another, my door is always getting closed.

I'm standing at the kitchen sink cupping water in my hands. I've been drinking Little Sokoki town water. The sleeves of my sweater are soaked.

I still have some choices. I can drown myself right now. Walk out my door and out of River House and into the Connecticut River. From there, who knows where the water will take me? Or I can, as most anyone would say, "pull up my socks."

I'm trying to choose the sock thing. After all, thoughts of death are easy, planning a death is easy—it's the execution that dims a person's enthusiasm.

How I shall die is clear enough: the look, if not the feel, of it. But what then? Go to my own funeral? Besides me, who else will come? The police and my agent? What will they say to each other? The press will be ravenous, cruel. Will my mother show up, will he? Will Kate? If so, then what?

Then what? I suddenly realize I believe in a "what." What is "what" like?

As bile rises in my throat, images of the usual heaven arise in my mind: a fundamentalist American heaven. Heaven is the ultimate bad movie. It's poorly imagined, poorly written, poorly dressed, poorly shot, and poorly scored. Plus there's only one star. With no plot, no romance, no conflict, all the idiot extras get to do is sing: Hosannah! Hosannah means "save me." By the time they get to heaven, aren't they saved? Or have they finally discovered that what they really needed saving from all along was their creation of heaven? Heaven is also way over budget. And forever.

I shy—violently. For now, to stay here, no

matter the cost, no matter how hellish, is preferable to going there.

Standing at my window, looking down into Main Street, I manage to find a nightlight in all this darkness. What if I'm not crazy? What if all these things are not my own personal movies? What if River House is haunted?

I hug myself.

Well, there you go. To save myself, I've walked onto the set of *The Shining*.

He was offered the lead in *The Shining*. That was years before my time. He turned it down. Too close, I think, to the bone. But he did do a small European film for Polanski that scared the hell out of me. It scared the hell out of everybody. At the time, it even scared the hell out of him. Very dark. Very bleak. Set in one storage room and the war-damaged main exhibition hall of an abandoned museum in late Forties Berlin. A young German girl was in it, very pretty, very talented, but she might as well have stayed in her dressing room. He carried the entire movie. He was brilliant. He was terrible in his brilliance. Was it called *The Curator*? I think it was called *The Curator,* but I can't really remember. Still, it's the movie that made me think of him when I was turning *The Windigo's Daughter* into a screenplay.

I've decided River House is haunted. There's no other explanation. Unless I'm crazy. I'm not crazy. I'm a writer. I live in worlds entirely of my own making, but I am not crazy. So River House is crazy. Houses can be crazy. Shirley Jackson said so and on the subject of haunted houses

Shirley Jackson was infallible. Hotels can be even crazier. Ask Stephen King. There's more to work with. More people have passed though leaving more psychic debris. River House is full of ghosts—though it seems only I can see them. Why me? Is it because, like Edith Wharton and Henry James haunting Edith's old mansion together in Lenox, Massachusetts, I am almost a ghost myself?

No. Hold on. I'll bet others see them. I'll bet there's more than one tenant of River House tormented by them, but like any self-respecting ghost-raddled soul, they're hiding it. Or, like me, they think they're going insane. And they're hiding that. Or, unlike me, they know quite well what's who, and who's what, but keep it to themselves for fear of scorn.

If there are others, even if it's only one other, there is safety in numbers.

I have something to do. I must add to my total sum of one. That "other" couldn't be Miss Jackson. It couldn't be Benjamin Willow. And it sure as hell couldn't be Lizard Woman who walks the halls by night. And by day if she feels like it. Of course! It's the young man with the apple. And the camcorder. And maybe a dog.

Life is an addiction. Once you get a taste for it, along about your third month in, it's almost impossible to stop doing it. Going to sleep, waking up, finding something to eat, drinking another cup of coffee, smoking another cigarette, hearing some more bad news, looking for love, looking for trouble, ticking off another list of "things to do today," writing another unremarkable book, another unremarkable screenplay, listening to the voice in your head that never never *never* stops talking long enough to let you, whoever you are, actually think. Or rather, feel.

Like a repentant junkie, I'm desperate to stop shooting up. Like an end-of-the-line drunk, I'd give anything to stop drinking. Like a lifer, I'd kill to get out of here. I want to be dead. I want to be where Kate is and if that's nowhere, then nowhere sounds like heaven to me. But like most junkies and most drunks and most lifers, I can't kick the habit. I'm scared. It hurts too much. I don't believe in hell, but what if DeMille is waiting for me? I haven't got the god-damned nerve. So—I'm still alive. Christ. It must have been the adrenaline, the running, the rush, that made me think I would write something worth the living. But I won't. Even if I could, I won't. So why haven't I done what Hunter Thompson did, phone in one hand, .45 caliber pistol in the other, and blown out my brains in the middle of a sentence? Asshole. Another asshole writer desperate for people to note his stupid selfish death, just like they watched his stupid selfish gonzo living. Thompson was talking to his wife. He blew out his brains as his last gift of love to someone who must have once loved him, who might still have been loving him as she heard the blast in her ear. God, I hate writers. I especially hate writers who kill themselves. The rest of us have to read all about it.

Thomas Wolfe once wrote: "At that instant he saw, in one blaze of light, an image of unutterable conviction, the reason why the artist works and lives and has his being—the reward he seeks—the only reward he really cares about, without which there is nothing. It is to snare the spirits of mankind in nets of magic, to make his life prevail through his creation, to wreak the vision of his life, the rude and painful substance of his own experience, into the congruence of blazing and enchanted images that are themselves the core of life, the essential pattern whence all other things proceed, the kernel of eternity."

There are those who say Wolfe did himself in. But they're wrong. The right side of his brain killed the man who wrote *Look Homeward, Angel.* It exploded one day, right there in his head.

He was right about writing. That's why I do it. To snare the spirits of mankind in nets of magic, to make my life prevail through what I make, to thrust myself into the core of dreaming Life with blazing and enchanted images.

Oh, right. As Dorothy Parker would say, as she *did* say, and I'm the Queen of Rumania.

Making my life prevail through what I make? If I could laugh, it would be one of those laughs writers call "bitter." As in: "Tell me another one," she laughed bitterly. (Of course, if I wrote a sentence like that, there'd be no adverb. I don't do adverbs. I might have written—and so might one of my writing heroes, Raymond Chandler, but he'd do so much better—"Tell me another one," she said, with a laugh as bitter as almonds.) Aside from my most recent mess, I've made a few other little prevailing messes along the way. None of them compare to the mess in Malibu, but they qualify as little cruelties just the same, or what the cartoonist-playwright Jules Feiffer (is he dead? has he killed himself yet?) called *Little Murders.* *Little Murders* begins with the Newquist family heaping unrelenting abuse on each other, continues for quite awhile in much the same horribly funny way, and ends when they finally begin gunning down passing pedestrians from their New York City apartment window.

Not entirely sure I'd fit in with the Newquist family, but I've had my little moments. For instance, I am twelve and my mother and I now live in Santa Rosa, California because one of her "boyfriends" has moved to Santa Rosa, California. I hate Santa Rosa. Yet again, halfway through a school year, I am introduced to a classroom of typical kids who've known each other since nursery school. Typical means some are nasty, a special few are very nasty, two or three are sweet to one degree or another, and the rest are just kids: totally preoccupied with their own problems, which at that age are truly painful...mostly because they've yet to complete the construction of their adult protective devices like denial and repression. For some reason, one of the nice ones takes to me. And I begin to play in her dark destruction of a house, a house called, quite rightly: The Shambles. I know this immediately because its name is carved on a wooden shingle nailed to a tree in the front yard. The important part of this story is that my friendly classmate has a five year old sister and whenever the little sister and I are alone together, I torture her: pinching her, dumping her in toy chests and sitting on the lid, tripping her up, whatever. I remember nothing about my new friend, but I've never forgotten the little sister.

Looking back, I suspect I carry a gene or two of those "special few." I also suspect the little sister was the model for *The Bad Seed*. Or was that me? It could have been the both of us, and I saw who she was because something in me knew who I was.

Be that as it may—

Throughout the years, I've cut off old friends without a word of explanation, made remarks biting enough to bring tears, felt nothing but irritation at the pain of others, read about the torture, slaughter, misery of millions with hardly a sigh, stolen a few things (like Winona Ryder, I got caught once or twice), and so far, I've never sent a single cent to a single charity anywhere. Why go on? These are not "blazing and enchanted images."

Who gives a shit if my life prevails?

I'll find the beautiful boy with the apple. He cares about me. I don't know why, but he does. He must be able to help.

Starting on the fifth floor, I can't find the boy. But I found the apple. Lying on the hallway carpet, I see it halfway down the High Street side of River House. I can't walk normally. I'm dizzy. Being dizzy, I use the wall to keep my balance as I walk towards the apple. It takes forever to reach the damn thing. I don't know why I bother. Apples can't talk. His apple isn't going to tell me which apartment is his, which door to knock on. No point even in making my way down to the lobby where the mailboxes are. There are names on each of the boxes. If I knew his name, I'd know his floor and the number of his apartment. I don't know his name.

The apple lies directly in front of apartment 5-4. Fifth floor, fourth apartment. Could it be his? Why not? It could be. And even if it isn't, maybe whoever lives there will know his name, his number.

I pick up the apple with my left hand, knock with my right.

The door is answered immediately. By the Incredible Scaling Woman. Before I can run, her hand reaches out and grips my wrist. She's strong. She's inhumanly strong. She's also maybe fifteen years old. "How sweet," she says, "You've returned my apple. Not many people would do that." And then with impossible strength she pulls me off my feet and into apartment 5-4.

The door slams behind us. There's no one there, but it slams anyway.

There must be a few dozen people in LA alone who hate me more than William Holden's character hated Grace Kelly's character most of the way through *The Country Girl*. And for much the same reason. Like Holden thought Kelly was the cause of her husband Bing Crosby's troubles, Hollywood thinks I am the source of my man's drinking. They think that without me, he could have stopped drinking, could have worked harder, been happier, found someone sweeter, prettier, younger, less competitive who would have fulfilled his real needs. They thought all this because, like the spineless character Crosby played, he flat out told them so, and he told them so because when Kate and I were gone in Tombstone, he was alone and he was lonely, but worse, he was scared. He couldn't be alone. He also told them because he was a conniving drunk. The man required twenty-four hour maintenance. It took me awhile, but I learned that his own company tormented him. Alone, his voices grew louder, uglier. His need for drink or sex or work grew stronger. Without a woman to hold him up, he needed his "good friends" around. For him, a good friend was anyone who would take his drunken calls in the middle of the night. A good friend was someone he could get to do all the things I usually did for him. And to get them to do that, he had to convince them they were vital to him, and that he was helpless. The real trick was to convince them that I was the witch who had stolen his soul. It was easy. People buy a story like that before it's half told...so it worked beautifully. After all, he was a great actor. And he really was in need.

There are those in Hollywood, most especially his oldest friend, a fairly decent character actor who only had work because he insisted on having him in all his pictures, who would push his way through a charge of rhinos to volunteer to inject the toxin at my execution.

No one in his movie and my movie ever played the part to the end. No one got as far as William Holden did when he discovered Grace Kelly was being used by a cunning drunk. Of course, I wasn't really Grace Kelly, although I was certainly used by a cunning drunk. In the end of *The Country Girl*, Kelly leaves Holden to remain with her drunk, played so well by Bing Crosby I'm damned sure he knew a thing or four about drinking. I imagine what we're supposed to think when Grace runs after Bing is that they live happily ever after.

Truth is, in the end of our movie, we all keep drinking until we die.

This is my movie and I don't think I'm going to have to kill myself. I think River House will do me the favor.

The woman, smaller now, and as said, much

younger, her features melting like hot wax and sliding towards the bottom of her face, still has a grip on my wrist. There's no fighting her. She's stronger than me. Her grip is like steel cuffs. When she tugs, I have to follow.

"Only naughty girls allowed," she says. I imagine she means me. I am, if nothing else, a first class naughty girl.

The day he died I'd spent the morning in the kitchen. By then, I was always in the kitchen. I was always cooking. Anything. Everything. As if by making food, serving food, I could stay in the center, in the warm. As if by preparing food, I could sustain things.

Food was life. I was trying to live. Kate was dead, but I was still trying to live.

Nothing was eaten. Not on that day. Not on the days that had passed since we buried her. Neither he nor I sat down to a meal I'd made. I don't know what he lived on—the olives in his martinis, probably. I must have survived on aroma.

But I went on cooking. I bought the food, I brought it home, I cooked it, I threw it away.

The day he died I was frying sea bass in a wok. The whole fish, head, tail, all of it. He hated fish, he especially hated sea bass but, really, how could that matter?

I hadn't seen him for days. If I slept at all, I slept alone. I cooked. He worked, soaked up gallons of Hollywood sympathy for his loss, came home and hid in his study, passed out on his couch. He drank.

When he stumbled through the kitchen door, I was standing at the butcher block in the bottom

half of a pair of his pajamas, a tee shirt that said
Road to Perdition (yet again, he'd been offered the
lead but was tied-up filming something else; we still
got a tee shirt, one for each of us), and white socks.
I was slicing red peppers, green peppers, yellow
peppers. Chef's knife in my hand, not looking up,
trimming, cutting, chopping, I knew exactly when
the wok caught fire. Naked and heading for the
fridge (more olives?), he'd slid on a slice of pepper
on the kitchen floor, or he was stung by something,
a bee or a wasp, or he just fell the fuck over as he
often did, and smashed into the stove. Usually
he missed everything, including his head on the
stone fireplace or the edge of the glass coffee table,
but this time he'd taken the sea bass with him.
He'd knocked the whole sizzling fish to the floor,
splattered his arms, his hands, his naked thighs,
his crotch, with hot oil.

There he was on the Spanish floor tiles, yelling,
cursing peppers, bees, the fish, God, me, and
thrashing at his legs with a dish towel. Above him,
the fire flared up in the wok, jumped from oily wok
to oily stove top, raced for the wall.

Knife in my hand, I chopped the peppers
smaller and smaller and smaller. Knife in my hand,
I chopped and chopped.

No use pulling, all I got for my struggling with
the girl in 5-4 was pain. I could, I thought, accept
dying, but I had no intention of getting hurt.
Already, it seemed as if her hand, the skin rough as
a file, was abrading my wrist. I thought of infection,
of Lovecraft, of ghosts. The woman was no ghost.
A demon perhaps, but nothing so insubstantial as a
shade of life lost but reluctant to leave.

I'd been pulled across the entire room, a room decorated as all the rooms of River House were: feature wall, yellow tiles, thin brown carpet, dark yellow kitchen. Another unfurnished room. Another room with a bath and a closet. This room faced out over the back parking lot. Unlike mine, it was perfectly square, perfectly ordinary, perfectly horrid.

We were heading for the closet.

"Where are we going?" I asked.

"Where else," she said in a dark brown voice, "to the stairs."

They blew the ashes of Hunter Thompson out of a canon taller than the Statue of Liberty. Perfect. Old Gonzo (I gag) shot from guns, a flaky load of dead writer. I hope he watched. I hope he stood there with all the other swollen gonads picking exploded gonzo out of their teeth. I hope Sylvia Plath was with him, wearing her oven like a hat. I hope Hemingway shook his shotgunned skull bones like hot dice. I hope he showed up—my man, always the ham, always the actor. If he made that special appearance, I'll bet he found his head. I'll bet he pushed his way down stage with it tucked under his arm.

Hanging out with his fellow flakes, I hope Hunter Thompson finally noticed what a meatball he really was. By which I mean, Thompson.

Thank whatever for the Girl Who Sheds. She is my salvation. I can't do this anymore. I can't keep this up. Nowhere to go, nothing to do, no one to be. Life is a dream and we are dreamers. I have nightmares, more and more of them, but dreams?

No dreams. No books, no scripts, no poems. "Are you nobody too?" No, Miss Dickinson, a strange and charmed singularity if ever there was one, I am not nobody too. I'm missing more than my body. I'm missing my soul.

It's late. It's dark. Too late and too dark to find the river. I'm not stuck with gassing myself in front of my kids, or blowing out my brains on the phone with my wife, and I sure as hell am not stumbling around in the dark trying to find the best spot to throw myself in a river. I could miss, land on a rock, break a leg. I could get stuck in mud, slowly sinking. I could get washed into the fish ladder, have the entire town of Little Sokoki rescuing me, make the front page of their local paper as an attempted suicide. Or a damned fool. No. No river after all. And no humiliating choice back in California: lethal injection or gas chamber. I shall die by stairs that exist or don't exist, but either way are the handiwork of every creative mind that's ever walked the halls of River House. Including mine.

As for who dreamed up Lizard Woman, if I had to guess, I'd guess—me. I'm the script writer here. I'm the low brow lowlife.

Another perk of death by imagination. No body. I'm not going to be found in my room. Or dredged up from the Connecticut River bottom.

I'm spared the fate of Parker. Dorothy Parker tried barbiturates a few times. All she got for her trouble was waking up with a thick crust of dried drool all down her chin and someone at her bedside staring in repelled horror. And when she finally did make it, what happened then? Undiscovered for weeks, rats nibbled at her fingers, her toes, her nose, her ears, her eyes. She must have made a revolting corpse. What if she'd had a gun? She could have missed, wound up a rutabaga. What if she jumped from a window, a window like my window? I once saw a retrospective screening of Roman Polanski's *The Tenant*. (Where was that? New York? London? Who cares?) Polanski's poor maddened tenant, driven to dress in drag, jumped in despair from his third floor window. He didn't die. Dripping with blood, dragging a shattered leg, he crawled all the way back up to his apartment— and jumped again. He still couldn't die. Even more bloody, even more broken, he lived, but not necessarily as himself. He lived as the eternal tenant doomed to constantly jump out the same window. A strange little movie of possession. But possession by what? Polanski never said.

Mine is also getting to be a rather strange little movie.

It really is time for the credits to roll. So okay, I'll climb the stairs with the wandering regressing girl. I shall be the idiot in the attic after all.

She's let go of my hand and disappeared. That's all right. I'll climb anyway.

This time the stairs are wide and shining with polish. They're carpeted: thick, nightdark, soundless. In the inward curve of each step there are brass stair clips. On one side is a wall of rich smooth paneling, on the other a carved handrail. Over the finely made rail I can look down into what seems a large sitting room, but only a small portion of it: one corner of a handsome wingback chair, a matching ottoman, the edge of a gorgeous Oriental rug, wine red, sea blue. Directly underneath me, there's a high glass dome covering a stuffed bird, an owl, I think. I can hear a fire crackle, the kind of fire contained in a fireplace. The glow from the unseen fire shines in the dead owl's dead eyes. Looking up, there's a high railed platform, above that an open window, and streaming in the window, terrifying moonlight.

I can't breathe. My knees hurt. The bones in my ankles, in my wrists, in my neck, hurt. I don't know my own name.

Why don't I know my name? I catch sight of my hand on the railing. I'm climbing the stairs in the great country house I've always dreamed about, the one I've always waited for (as I know it has always been waiting for me), and I see that my hand is fat. That my arm is fat. I hadn't known I was fat. I stop. Look down at myself. Oh yes, I'm fat all right. I'm more than fat. I'm obese. Over my immensity, I'm wearing a huge dress like the dress Stevie Smith once wore, its fabric smothered in flowers. Stevie called it her "they all came up" dress. It's not my dress. It can't be. I wouldn't wear a dress like this. Would I?

Mother wouldn't be seen dead in it. Mother wouldn't allow me to be seen dead in it. So, why am I wearing it? Is it because Mother's dead? A little voice, certainly not mine, whispers: "I hope so."

It's taking an age to get up these stairs. After every step, I must stop and catch my breath, push my glasses back up my sweaty nose, hold my fat hand over my fat heart, stand there wheezing and aching and dying for a drink, for a cigarette. The liquor's in the kitchen, but I promise myself a cigarette when I get to the platform at the top of the

stairs. I comfort myself with the knowledge that
there's half a pack of Pall Malls in a pocket of this
huge flowery dress. My pills are in another pocket.
I call them "mother's little helpers." I can't imagine
life without my pills.

Wheezing, muscles trembling with effort, the
pain in my knees, my ankles almost unbearable, it
takes me what seems like forever, but I get there,
I make it to the window. Fumbling in my pocket
I find the lighter to light my cigarette. Fingers
shaking, heart fluttering in my chest, I inhale: pah!
Practically cough up my lungs. I can't breathe,
but I certainly can smoke. But there, it's working.
I'm calmer, feeling a little better already. Heart is
slowing, my throat is opening up. Up here I can
lean my bulk against the railing, take some of
the terrible weight off my tormented feet. Puffing
away, I look out the window. Directly below,
there's a circular drive. Sweeping round the front
of the house, it leads to a straight road lined either
side with dark trees: tall, fully leafed out oaks or
beech. Whatever they are, their trunks are thick
with age. I must be right above the front entrance
because even from this far up, I hear it when the
door suddenly slams. A young woman has come
running out from under the peaked roofing over
the door. I see her race for a small car parked
apart from a group of other cars. As if running
from savages, she throws herself into it and guns
away from my house, gravel spraying up, hind-end
fishtailing. Behind her, another young woman has
just appeared from under the roof, immediately
followed by a young man. Both of them are
sprinting after the car, both shouting. They're
calling a name. They're calling, "Eleanor! Eleanor!"

The second young woman is screaming, "Don't leave, please, Eleanor, don't go!" But "Eleanor" already has her little car halfway to the drive that runs between the dark trees.

I'm fascinated now. The air around my head grows thick with smoke. I breathe easily. I don't feel my weight. Nothing hurts. I have no thoughts about Stanley, about Mother, about our wicked North Bennington neighbors. It's as if I have no thoughts and no body at all. I am nothing but a thing that watches.

An older man has pelted down the drive after the two young people running after Eleanor. But none of them can outrun a car. None of them can get anywhere near a car being driven as this one is driven. Eleanor is steering at speed straight down the middle of the tree lined driveway, when suddenly—no hesitation, no braking, no swerving at the last moment—the little car lurches to the right, and smashes headlong into one of the trees, one of the huge implacable trees.

Someone's knocking on my door. Far far away, I hear it...pounding now, not knocking. If it's that goddamned walking scaly lizard of a girl, I swear I'm punching her right in the nose, psoriasis be damned.

I get down the stairs a lot faster than I got up, yank open my door, fist up and ready. My fist isn't fat. My hands, my legs, my ass, my tits, my belly, pendulous with fat a moment ago, are all thin. Actually, if I got any thinner, I might not have to jump out a window. I could just sit in a corner and waste away. No tented dress of Stevie Smith's entire flower garden hanging down below my knees;

I'm wearing his pajama bottoms and a sport's bra.

It's Miss Jackson. It's the manager of River House. My god, have I left the door to the closet open?

For a change, I wasn't stupid. For once, I managed to be uncharacteristically sly. I took off the clothes I'd been wearing, everything, even the clasp in my hair, stuffed it all into a black plastic bag, stuffed the plastic bag into a big leather bag. I left the cars, both in my name since he did not drive. No taxi, no limo, no borrowing a neighbor's car, no taking my motorcycle or either of the mountain bikes (he did occasionally ride a bike), no hitchhiking. In dark and sensible clothes, sturdy and sensible hiking shoes, and a knitted hat hiding my hair, I walked away from the burning house straight down the winding canyon road into Malibu, two miles or more. All I carried was my laptop in its case and the big leather bag slung over my shoulder. In the leather bag were the remaining shreds of my life: the extreme minimum of clothing, a few photos, all of them Kate, a few letters, a few books (one of them called *Movie Money: Understanding Hollywood's (Creative) Accounting Practices*, 2nd Ed.), a couple of important papers (might come in handy, might not), a few valuables for possible, though not probable, pawning, the black plastic bag—plus some extra special extra damaging evidence sealed in a jar, then sealed again in a freezer baggie. When the shrieking police cars and clanging fire trucks raced the other way, I faded into the bushes at the side of the road.

In Malibu, I meant to empty my bank account, not his (no touching his money, not if I wanted to retain some small love for myself), but as luck would have it a cop car was sitting right in front of the Wells Fargo bank, no cop in the car, but the engine running (why wasn't it racing to my house? everyone else was), so I kept on walking. All the way to Santa Monica.

People do walk the Pacific Coast Highway, admittedly not rich people, not even middle class people. Cher, apparently under the risible impression no one recognizes her, actually jogs it in huge sweats and a fright wig. Everyone says: "Oh look, there goes Cher again." But on that particular day I looked nothing like Cher, especially under that hat. He hated the hat. I hated the hat. But Kate had pointed to it in a shop, cried until I bought it. Kate loved the hat. Too big for her, she wore it everywhere she toddled. The day she died I found it caught up in the oleander bushes before I found her.

It's eight miles on the ocean side of the PCH from "downtown" Malibu to Santa Monica's California Incline, and no one looked at me twice. Adrenalin can do that, can keep you going way past your usual limits. I stopped only once to duck down onto the beach. Hidden by rocks from all but crabs and seagulls and pelicans, I cut my credit cards into tiny pieces, buried the pieces deep under one of the biggest rocks, one that wasn't going anywhere and was never washed by the tide.

Somewhere on Ocean Avenue, I hopped the first of the city buses that eventually took me to Union Station where I bought a bus ticket to Sacramento. Why Sacramento which meant nothing to me? Because the bus for Sacramento was leaving in three and a half minutes and unless you're crossing into Mexico or Canada, buses don't ask for an id.

After three changes, and eight hours from LA to Sacramento on one bus or another, I knew where I was going. I was going to a palace in Vermont; I was going to what I thought of as "home."

In Sacramento, I spent the night in a Motel 6, one near a supermarket. Before I checked in, cash only, I checked if it had a hotplate. It did. At the supermarket, I bought what I needed. In the motel, besides trying to sleep, I did what I had to do. In the morning, I caught a Greyhound to Springfield, Massachusetts. If I hadn't already been in hell, I would have been in hell. Six transfers, three round-the-clock days. In Springfield, I waited forty eight more cautious hours in a cheap hotel watching TV. Amidst all the abject nonstop crap, not to mention seeing his face (and occasionally mine) on every major news program, I caught a late-night showing of *Thelma and Louise*. I must have taken three pages of notes watching that one. Don't talk to anyone. Don't invite anyone into your motel room. No matter who they are, don't tell anyone even the tiniest detail about yourself. Don't make phone calls. Not even to someone who loves you and wishes you only the best. That last one was easy to avoid doing. I killed the only person I wanted to call. And he killed the only other person I'd call even if she could only talk baby talk.

I bought newspapers, read about the Malibu fire, about the tragic death of a much loved movie star, about the movie star's missing wife, a novelist and screenwriter, about how the movie star and his wife had recently suffered the loss of their only child, about how the police were co-operating coast-to-coast in an effort to find the wife "for questioning."

131

In Springfield, walking the narrow junked-out streets just to be moving after all that sitting and all that TV, I passed a gang of Homies rollin' on E and burning godswot in an oil drum. No complaints when I wordlessly tossed in my black plastic bag. It hurt, but I also threw in Kate's beloved hat. The wool made a horrible stink; they loved it. Then I caught my last bus. I paid for a ticket to Montreal, Canada, but I got off way before that—I got off in Little Sokoki, Vermont.

I'm not afraid of Miss Jackson anymore. When you're dead, you don't have to say you're sorry. What the hell does she want? What's she doing knocking on doors at this time of night? What's that stupid look on her face? Has she come to offer me an apple?

Since I say nothing and since she says nothing, expecting me, no doubt, to start whatever she's come to finish, we both stand there looking at each other. I've never really looked at Miss Jackson before. She looks like a character actress I know, always in work because every movie calls for some woman with a sharp nose and a sharper tongue making trouble for the lead and/or leads.

This is my movie. I'm the lead. She's the character actress in a small speaking role. I'll listen to her do her thing, and then get back to whatever the hell I was doing. What was I doing? Was I writing? Drinking? Following the walking woman up a new and unusual set of stairs? Hoping she meant to kill me? Or herself? Or both of us? Were there two of us? Has there ever been two of us? I remember one thing very clearly. I was fat. Women don't miss things like that. Miss Jackson? Mrs. Jackson. Jackson! I remember. What I was doing

132

was dreaming I was Shirley Jackson who had grown fat from too much food and wheezy from too many cigarettes and cagey from too much drink. Shirley was dreaming her own book. She was living in *The Haunting of Hill House.* Or I was.

I slam the door on Miss Jackson. I have to get back to the stairs.

Comes a tremendous blam on the door. I hesitate. Miss Jackson obviously has something to say to me. Just as obviously I couldn't give a rat's turd for whatever it might be. And yet, I can't lose my apartment. I can't lose my stairs.

Arranging my face, I open the door again.

"Sorry. Didn't mean that. Yes?"

Even now, Miss Jackson wants to draw it out, whatever it is. We're back to staring at each other. I win. Miss Jackson says, "There have been complaints."

No way I'm sleeping in a cardboard box on the riverbank. No way I'm leaving River House. So I say (rather nicely), "Oh dear. Really?"

"Really."

Miss Jackson is trying to see into my room. "What do they tell you I've done?" I ask, moving toward her, blocking more of my door, making her take a step back.

"Where do I start," she says, obviously furious I've forced her small retreat.

She wants prompting? Sorry. She's on her own here. I move even closer, which allows me to almost, but not quite, shut my door.

"First of all," she says, taking yet another deeply resented step back, "There's been a lot of loud banging from your room. The man below you can't sleep."

I look sorry about that.

"You were also seen running up and down the stairs in the middle of the night. You scared the handicapped woman in 2-7."

I am sorry about that too, but I am moved to say, "I had a reason."

"Yes? And that reason would be what?"

"The same reason I had when I came to your office to do some complaining of my own. Someone pounds on my door at all hours of the night. I wasn't running up and down the stairs for nothing. I was chasing her to the second floor."

Miss Jackson's turn to say, "Really?"

"Really. You and Benjamin Willow rent to some very odd people, Miss Jackson. I am far from the oddest."

It's true. Considering the state of River House, she rents to whomever she can: people on Section Eight, people on drugs, a few who sell drugs, seven illegal Thais in one room working the Thai restaurant on High Street, more than a few drunks, a recluse who fills his apartment with fruit, single moms with neglected kids, a woman who keeps loose rabbits and one loose tortoise in her studio apartment, an old man who abuses his much older wife, the handicapped woman in apartment 2-7. Her "handicap" is that she's even more loopy than the average River House tenant. Although it might actually be true that I am the oddest.

"You're talking about the woman you think lives here?"

"I bloody am. As for the man below me, I'm sorry. I'll be quieter. But lady, you have someone who gets into this building whenever she feels like it, and she feels like it a lot. I have no idea if she's bothering anyone else, but she's driving me out of my mind."

Miss Jackson gives me a look which leaves me in no doubt that she thinks I'm out of my mind alright and that her building has nothing to do with it. "There is no woman who comes here."

"Tell her that."

We stand there some more; by now I'm practically in the hallway, my door practically shut, and Miss Jackson practically unmanned. Or whatever. I think I'm getting scarier. Hair, skin, weight, fingernails, eyes, mouth, teeth: all of them less and less healthy, more and more unpleasant.

"And finally," she finally says, "I'm told you're keeping a dog in your room."

That one gets me. That complaint actually stuns me. Dog? I have no dog in my room, and I say so, very clearly. From the moment I met her, Miss Jackson has pissed me off—so I really need the last word. "Not only is there no dog in my room and not only is there some fruit-and-nutcase pounding on my door at all hours, but do you ever get complaints about bothering people in their rooms so late at night?"

"No. Especially since it's four fourteen in the afternoon."

I don't want to. I try not to. But my head turns towards the window. Sky as blue as blue sky.

Like the dog she hopes I have, Miss Jackson bares her teeth. Tiny teeth, like seed pearls. Disturbing teeth. By now, though, I am not one to speak. "If I do find out you're keeping a dog, it's grounds for immediate eviction."

"No dog."

Her eyes slide around me to my door. To the tiny crack of its opening. I can almost hear her thoughts. If there's a dog inside, its nose would be behind that crack doing what doggie noses do: trying to sniff her out. No nose. No sound of sniffing. She's disappointed.

I say, "Are you by any chance related to Shirley Jackson?"

"Who?"

How wonderful. Someone else who does not read. "Never mind."

I hate to give it to her. She walks away like a panther. I once said, "Hell is other people." Then I was told Sartre said it too, not only before me, but in French. "L'enfer, c'est les autres." Great existentialists think alike.

I know something Miss Jackson doesn't know. Four fourteen in the afternoon is when I found Kate in her drowning pool.

I'm sitting on the toilet when I remember what I'd been doing. And who I'd been doing it with. The girl who doesn't live here, and perhaps doesn't live at all, at least not in the usual way of things, that girl and I were going walkies together. Up or down the stairs, not sure which. And then I became Shirley Jackson in the process of dreaming up *The Haunting of Hill House* until the other Ms. Jackson who also haunts River House, came knocking on my door. And now I'm peeing. If nothing else, I can pee. I can still do that.

No point trying to write. Even if I do manage a few words, they won't be there next time I look. Besides, I think by now it's obvious I won't be writing a book or a screenplay to leave behind. I

don't know why I even wanted to. Who is there left
to care what I do or I don't do? There's only me,
and I don't care enough about myself to brush my
own teeth. But here's the fucking kicker: no matter
how frightened I am, no matter how useless the
outcome, no matter I'm pushing my luck with the
cops, I have decided to live a few more days. I need
to know about the stairs in the back of my closet.
I need to know who the girl is, or what she is. I
need to know about the stories that haunt River
House, or if they don't haunt River House—if they
only haunt me. And if I am haunted by the stories
of other artists, much better artists, artists who've
walked the halls of River House when it was still a
hotel, still a child's haunted palace, I need to know
why. Most of all, I need to know why I can't be
haunted by stories of my own.

Sitting here peeing, I've come to my senses. If
I ever did, I no longer want to throw myself out of
the tower. Landing would be a terrible, and very
public Brautigan quality, mess. It might hurt. Like
Polanski's Tenant, I might not die immediately. I
might lie there pulped on the sidewalk, looking
up at faces looking down, faces full of horror and
of pity, faces full of outrage to have their day so
marked, faces trying not to puke. Under all those
faces, looking up all those noses, in my death scene
I might make a scene dying. I have more style left
than that. Certainly more vanity.

I came here to die gracefully in the beautiful
river. But I won't. However it happens, no matter
how I work it, it'll all be pathetic. Dead bodies are
pathetic. They're laughable. People make jokes
about them: coroners, mortuary staff, doctors,
nurses, lab technicians, cops—unless they happen

to know they're near someone who knew the deceased and gives a shit. The only dead bodies people respect are the bodies of children. Dead children bother people.

All my corpse will do is create headlines and stories that get wilder and wilder and farther and farther from the truth of what I was. No one will care why I killed him. All they'll care about is *how* I killed him and what I did with his body. Dennis Nielsen explained all that. Sad and lonely Dennis, living all by himself in his sad and lonely north London flat. Dennis killed for company. He'd learned if he allowed a guest to leave, they never came back. They never became his friend. So he killed them so they wouldn't leave. Problem was, after a bit of sitting around with them, dressing and washing them, putting them to bed like big soft Ken dolls, they'd begin to decompose and he'd be left with the bodies. What to do? Dennis wasn't whatisname, Eddie Gein. He wasn't much of an interior decorator so had little need for skin-of-human lampshades. Decomposing bodies were just so much garbage to get rid of. Yet when he was caught, which he might never have been if he hadn't lived in a flat on the top floor of a small house in a dense neighborhood of small houses, all anyone and everyone wanted to know was: what did he do with the bodies? They wanted to know how he'd cut them up and where. How he stored them under his floorboards. How he flushed them piece after piece down his loo. Not one of them cared *why* he did it. To a man (and woman, no doubt) they wanted only to hear *how* he did it.

For a serial killer, Dennis was rather sensitive. Sitting in prison, overnight a household name, he

138

finally understood his fellow man. If he'd known before he got started what he learned once he was caught, he might never have longed for a friend at all.

Like a returning queen, Faye walks up her own red brick path to her own house, a bride at last.

But as she walks, she sniffs at the air. Eyes the little brown saltbox house, the little brown woodshed, the small second-growth woods to either side. Where are the bees? The bluebottle flies? Will a cat leap out of a tree to arch its back and hiss? A dog call her names? Will Mrs. Wheelock's goat stick its head over the rail fence between her house and Mrs. Wheelock's house to blat insults?

No bees, no flies, no cat, no dog, no goat. Faye grins like a wolf grins. It doesn't really matter if a woolly mammoth is sitting out of sight round back on a lawn chair declaiming Hiawatha. *It's too late now. She can't be stopped. Faye is a married woman.*

The wedding guests stream through the gate on West Hackmatack Street, eager to follow Mr. Honig as he leads them onto the brick path that winds amongst the trees and finishes up at the lawn back of Faye's house. There's the open tent with the striped awning; there's the long table with the pink cloth. There's all the food. And there are the caterers: two young women with bobs and one young man with a pony tail who between them have set out the wedding feast and are now waiting to serve it. Mr. Honig has made all the arrangements with the caterers as well. Mr. Honig has thought of everything.

Although there is no band playing The Night We Were Wed, *there is a CD player on a long extension cord that is emitting something equally suitable. Faye doesn't know and doesn't care what it is. Mr. Honig has chosen the music. It may be Mrs. Honig's wedding, but it's Mr. Honig's reception.*

After everyone's taken the edge off their hunger and what eating is still being done is being done for the sheer greed of it, Mr. Honig gently taps a champagne glass with the edge of a cake knife. "My friends," he says, and everyone hushes like nightfall hushes a hive.

Faye, in her wedding dress—but no stockings and no shoes; she's kicked them off somewhere—settles herself on a lawn chair as far from her guests and the sugar maple saplings as she can get. The red of her dress is like a warning. Yet she yawns as if she had all the time in the world. Which she doesn't. Not if she wants to make the Vermont border by the setting of the sun. Which she does. But there's time and enough to spare for Mr. Honig's reception. She owes him that much for taking her away. Faye's eyeballs suddenly shift in their sockets—what's that! There's something in the hemlocks that grow on Mr. Hunnicutt's side of the back fence. Faye sniffs. But all she can smell are her wedding guests. Whatever it is, if she had her slingshot, she'd shoot it. But that would be a mistake...and so far, Faye is sure she's made

no mistakes.
Tempted, she's reasonably glad her
slingshot wouldn't fit under her dress.

I go to someone else's movie. It's late in the
afternoon, crisp as a cracker and yellow as butter.
The leaves are turning. Little Sokoki burns bright
in the falling sun. It seems only yesterday that
summer still idled against the walls, sat on public
benches, lay on the grass, trying to catch its breath.
Literally, only yesterday.

There's a small queue outside the River House
Theater. Is it Saturday? Am I attending a matinee?
No one holds the hand of a child. There are no
teenagers in the line. I think: maybe it's that rare
thing, a movie for grown-ups. I will lose myself
in a movie, calm myself down. I know movies. I
understand movies. If I watch someone else's
movie for an hour or two, I won't have to watch
mine.

I take my place in the line.

It's not until the titles roll that I know what
I'll be watching. The town-city of Little Sokoki is
having a Hitchcock festival. I've walked into *The
Lady Vanishes.*

Sitting in the dark, eating an enormous bag
of hot buttered popcorn, I am almost comforted. I
am on a train hurtling through a seventy year gone
Europe. I have nothing to do but watch. No one
knows who I am and I know no one. There really *is*
comfort in all this. No one sees the flames behind
my eyes; no one hears the screaming or smells
the blood. No one knows how she looked, her
small perfect body floating face down in peagreen

pondweed, small perfect goldfish nibbling at her fingers. No one knows what's in my leather bag. I am alone in here, under my skull, buried in bone. I am hidden. I am safe.

When the movie ends, I take a small portion of my comfort with me as I walk to the library to sit in a large fat library chair, and all around me are books about ghosts and hauntings. So far, I've learned five things. One: there is no real proof that ghosts actually exist. Two: there is no real proof that ghosts do not exist. Three: an amazing amount of people believe in them. Four: no two ghosts are alike. Five: you can know too much about a thing, namely ghosts, thereby end up knowing nothing about ghosts at all.

And then I walk "home" in the gathering dark.

I find myself walking slower and slower. Walking slower still, I'm trembling. There is no one near me, no one looking at me. No car has braked as it passes, no grim faces peer out behind thick glass. And I realize as I search for these things, that I am not afraid of the police. Or that I *am* afraid of the police—but I am much more afraid of River House. I am afraid of my room. I am afraid of my laptop.

Fucking artists. If failure doesn't kill us, success does. And if we manage to withstand what success does to us (one example of the many many examples who fail success: Norman Mailer, ace asshole, now finally shut up by death, at least here, in this reality), then curiosity is bound to bring us down in the end. Because curiosity keeps us working. Curiosity is at the root of all creativity. We have to know things, even if only how the story turns out.

Even when Kate died, he kept working. Less than a week after she drowned, he accepted a role: small budget film, quickly shot, he played a compulsive gambler with a seven year old son. The son lived alone in East LA motel rooms watching TV and eating takeout while Daddy went to the track day after day to try and beat the odds. And then out again at night for floating poker games. Brilliant movie. Heartbreaking movie. If he'd lived, he was up for another Best Actor Golden Globe. And if he got the Globe, why not another Oscar? Although, really, the movie seemed to me to be more about the boy than it was about him. For me, it was about the beauty and innocence of this child's inner world while Daddy's inner world was all about the ugliness of greed and the madness of the compulsive thrill of risk. (Called *Cheat the Devil*, it's playing now; it's playing all over the country to packed houses. People are coming out to see his last movie. Which means the first time producers are raking it in; for them, his death is a windfall, a monumental "lucky break.")

But me, I couldn't write, I couldn't eat, I could hardly breathe. All I could do was cook what no one ate. He went off to work each morning and became someone else, someone with a character arc. And then he came home each night and became himself. A flatline drunk and a babykiller.

If I'm to live as long as it takes to get up those stairs, I need to eat. A pain in the ass, but there it is. Time to walk to Price Chopper again. Very very slowly. The body gets weak lying around hallucinating. Or having visions. Or visitations.

Whatever.

I love the name. Price Chopper. Chop. Chop.

Life is here today, then gone, it seems—forever.
Even the rare: those with ineluctable ability or a
sublime gift or undaunted courage or unutterable
compassion...where does such genius go?
Christopher Reeve died. When it happened, I saw
it in a paper someone was reading at a checkout.
Christopher died. First he suffered. Then he
stopped suffering. I hope.

People die. They go away somewhere, or they
go nowhere, and they don't come back, while the
rest of us, all still living to one degree or another,
take it, and take it, and take it. We're here and we
really have no idea if there's a "there." And we lose
people like Reeve with floods of newsprint and then
a fading away, a fading away, as if he never was.
In ten years, in five, how many will ask: who was
Christopher Reeve?

Dylan Thomas demanded that we rage at the
dying of the light. And I do rage. I do. But not for
my light.

Once before, I'd entrusted him with Kate. It
was during one of his "bouts of sobriety." He was
in the midst of making a semi-independent movie
about Charles Lindbergh, aging from a shy yet
confident twenty-five year old to a defensive yet
confident seventy-two, from the dashing young icon
of the Twenties and Thirties, to the controversial
fallen hero he is now.

That one should have won him his first Oscar,
but the Oscars are political, and the US was, and
is, still slightly in love with Lucky Lindy. There was

a minor national outrage when the story suggested Lindbergh had had a hand in the death of his own child—an accidental hand, true, but stemming from his own bullying nature. Which was then covered up, and then—amazing happenstance—ferociously pinned on some poor schmuck who'd had the very bad idea of sending Lindy a ransom note. Hideous luck for the schmuck, but incredible luck for Lindbergh. (In the scriptwriter's opinion, unvoiced in his script, this was the genesis of the name Lucky Lindy.) Even worse, everyone hated to learn of Lindbergh's ties to Hitler and his belief that "inferior" people: criminals, the insane, and certain "races," ought to be "eliminated." This was voiced in the script. No wonder no one gave him an Oscar for that one. The academy flushed the whole movie: director, scriptwriter, cinematographer, actors, producers, whoever and whatever, down their private loos.

I loved that movie. He loved making it. We were in love with him and with me and with movies and with Kate. So I left him one evening to watch her. Where did I go? What was I doing? I haven't the foggiest. If anything, it must have had something to do with my own career. About that time, I was writing a very promising script for a young and very promising actress...until the night she died of an overdose on the dance floor of a popular nightclub on the Strip, and the whole thing died with her.

When I got home Kate was in tears. The whites of her eyes were red as blood. Turns out he'd given her a bath, no harm in that, but he'd washed her hair with a strong medicated shampoo. Stuff got in her eyes and she'd screamed and screamed,

screamed long enough and loud enough to bring in the neighbors. Who went away shaking their heads at how foolish some dads can be, poor man.

I said: that was a stupid thing to do. He said: how was I to know? I said: common sense. He said: I am far from common. Since Kate had forgiven him, and by now was happily nestled in his lap, I forgave him too. And we laughed at his folly. Kate laughed as well.

There is nothing more beautiful than the laugh of a child.

The girl is in the elevator. I'm on the ground floor with a plastic grocery bag in each hand; I've pushed the call button with my elbow, and when the elevator door opens—there she is, staring at me. Terrible to see her, but I try to be generous enough to feel heartened at the condition of her skin. It is less ravaged than the last time I was so close to her. She's so much younger now, she's merely a child. Beside her sits the dog who sat by the beautiful young man with the camcorder, the dog who stared at me in the parking lot behind River House the night I walked home alone. Dogs aren't allowed in River House. Miss Jackson made sure I saw that clause in my lease. Signing, I barely took note. I don't have a dog. No dogs since Prince. No desire for a dog since Prince. She's also posted a sign behind plexi-glass in the lobby. **No Dogs**, it says, **Infraction of this Rule is Grounds for Eviction**. This dog has a piteous case of mange. I can see the blood on his back where he's chewed the skin raw. He's cleaner. I think he might be black. Prince was black, but much smaller than this dog.

I am so shocked by both dog and the almost

child: prettier, cleaner, I think my heart actually
stops. Then starts. Then stops again. Then starts.
And I'm trying to back up fast, tripping over my
own feet, turning to get away. I'm not psychic. If
I were psychic I should never have gone off that
day, never have left my baby, my only Kate, in his
care. But I feel psychic now. There's a malevolence
flowing out of the elevator as a river of blood
flowed out of Kubrick's elevator in the lobby of the
Overlook Hotel. So I run. Not outside. Not out of
River House. For the stairs. The real stairs. I run
for the stairs because something makes me think I
can beat both of them to the third floor. Something
makes me think I'd better beat them to my door or
River House is going to kill me before I can do it for
myself.

I'm taking a shower. I can't recall when I last
took a shower. Looking down the length of my
dwindling body, watching the hair grow on my legs
and under my arms—damn, a person shaves for
years, as soon as she sees the first sprigs of body
hair somewhere in her early teens, so she never
even guesses at bottom she's actually the wife of
Bigfoot.

I have a rash on my thighs, on my stomach, my
toenails could use clipping. I know I won't bother
shaving or clipping or tweezing, though I do wash.
Then I get dressed for whatever comes next: pair of
now baggy old jeans, old sweater (black turtleneck),
white socks, sturdy brown walking shoes.

I'm lying on my futon again. It's come down
to this. Locking my door, gnawing a little cheese,
drinking a lot of wine, laptop on the foot of the
bed: unopened, unbooted, unused. I'm waiting for

the signal to enter my closet and climb the stairs. There's always a signal of some sort. Light. Music. Knocking. Banging. I've already removed my big bag, all the ceiling tiles, used my Price Chopper flashlight to look through the hole I've made in the back wall of the closet. Right at this moment, there are no stairs. There's no room for stairs. No room for anything but ancient (and no doubt poisonous) insulation, ancient lathing, dust, filthy cobwebs, and the double layer of old bricks that are the backside of the outside walls. Shining the light up: nothing but more of the same. Shining it down: more of the same. But something will happen, even if only in my head. It's entirely possible my head is where all the action is. But that's the artist for you.

I'm not tired. I'm not much of anything at all... except numb. In Malibu, before the beginning of the end, I was a terrible mother. Gone half the time, distracted when I was home, irritable, frantic, important. But I loved Kate with all my Houdini heart. Now I don't love anything, least of all myself. Yet I cannot stop the artist in me, cannot stop wanting to know, to make, to find out, to express.

What asses we are.

I don't understand. I've just snorted myself awake and where am I now? I'm in the movie theater under River House. Did I get here through my closet, by climbing, not up, but down the stairs? Old stairs, new stairs, a ladder? I have no idea. No dust, no cobwebs on my black sweater. I remember no dream. Perhaps this is my dream.

Much more of this and something will break. He once said his cracks were showing. My cracks aren't just showing, they're exposing themselves.

148

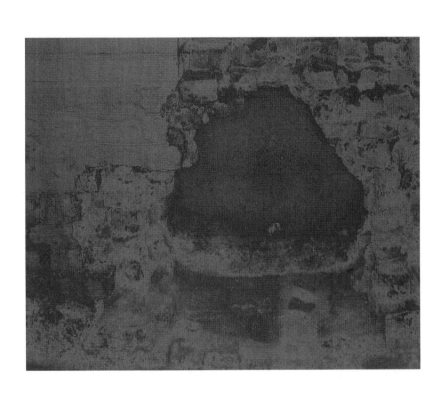

The stained silver screen is blank. I'm sitting here alone, clamped to my seat. On either side of the theater, just as they were when I saw *The Lady Vanishes*, there are faux grottos, faux porticos, faux staircases leading into or out of walls. Behind all these are distant views of painted vineyards. Weaving through this awkward excess, nymphs and satyrs frolic, tra la. It's meant to be Greek.

Twenty feet above me, the plastered Greek thing meets the Astrological thing. High overhead the ceiling is a blotchy teal blue and on it, rendered in flat white paint, wheels a badly drawn Zodiac.

For a moment, I touch an old self, a someone I once was; someone who laughed and caused others to laugh. For a moment he is here, sitting beside me, looking up and laughing. His laugh was cause for laughter. His laughter buoyed the heart.

For a moment, I am not who I've become.

For one single moment.

I think: *The Last Ditch* must be behind one of these tipsy walls.

Fuck. The laughter I almost laughed is coughed away like dust in the throat. I am not alone. My madly buoyed heart comes lose, bobs in waves of tossing fear. Ten rows in front of me, unmoving and silent, sits the old woman who became a young woman who has become a small child. She has turned in her seat; she's staring at me.

I should get up now. Walk out of the theater. I should turn my back on the hall-walker, the door-knocker, the body shrinker, the age reverser. In a minute I could be back out on the main street of Little Sokoki. From there, it's five minutes to the bus stop. If it's too late for a bus, it's fifteen minutes to the only interstate in Southern Vermont. I have a thumb. Moving fast and moving far, I could put all this, whatever it is, behind me. Problem is, my things are in my room. What little money I have left is in my room. The big bag is in my room—and what's worse, what is in the big bag is in my room.

Or maybe I should simply wake up.

No matter what, I have to get back to my room.

I stand. Like a crab, I begin to move sideways, inching myself out of my row, seat by seat, turning towards the exit. And there's the dog. It's the same dog, though a smaller dog than he was in the elevator. He's standing at the back of the theater, between me and the door into the lobby and from the lobby into the street. Once again, he has blood on his teeth.

The emergency exit is to my left and behind me. It's under a false staircase, and to get to it, I don't need to go anywhere near the child or the dog.

I'm out of my aisle and moving fast. The red of the exit sign is everything to me now. Nothing else exists but EXIT. Nothing.

Slamming my free hand against the release bar, I push open the door and am out. Out where there are stairs to climb. And I do climb, though these are not so much stairs as they are a fire escape behind the theater's screen. There's a movie flickering through it and I know immediately what it is. He loved James Whale. He loved Charles Laughton. The James Whale movie now playing features Charles Laughton. If I weren't so bloated with fright, I'd be pleased at my hallucinatory choice of *The Old Dark House*. The scratchy black & white film has reached that great moment when Boris Karloff, rampaging around drunk, has released the mad brother from where the other, madder, characters have caged him, and this brother sets the gloomy old pile on fire.

The man who made *Frankenstein* and *The Bride of Frankenstein* as well as *The Dark Old House* drowned himself in his own Hollywood swimming pool even though he was afraid of water. The note he left behind said, "The future is just old age and illness and pain. I must have peace and this is the only way."

No really going out, there's only a going up, and the farther up I go, the more unstable the fire escape. I'm scaling an outside wall of River House and I feel like Dracula scaling his castle walls.

I am insane. This is insanity. Or am I asleep dreaming I am insane? Waking up in bed, waking up in an empty movie house...have I ever really woken up? I don't understand what is happening to me, what's been happening since I took a room in River House. I had an idea. It isn't working. I have no ideas left. Except one. I could go to the police, give myself up. Could it be worse than what I do now? Horror stories make some kind of sense. There's a monster of some sort. An infinite variety of monsters. In horror stories you either get eaten by the monster or you defeat the monster. Ghost stories have their own kind of sense. Something truly haunts a place. Or it haunts a person. A demon, the newly dead, a force, usually ill intended. But this story makes no sense at all. Unless somewhere along the way I died. Maybe on the bus. Or in Springfield. Maybe the homies killed me for what little money I had. Maybe I never left Malibu. Maybe I died in the fire that didn't kill him—*I* killed him—but did get rid of our house and all we'd ever had together.

So, like the unnamed killer in Flann O'Brien's *The Third Policeman*, perhaps I'm in hell. The killer's soul is named Joe. I'm not as funny as Joe. Or as lucky in my companions. I get the Lizard Baby Woman and some stairs. And then there's the dog.

It's beginning to rain.

He met my mother just before she died. She had no idea she'd be dead in three days; that a very small time bomb was ticking away in the femoral artery of her left leg. All she knew was that I'd married a movie star. Not about to share her moment, she told no one we were coming to visit. If she had, her little apartment over a San Rafael, California, grocery store would have been wall to wall with co-workers, neighbors, regulars she drove in her cab. She made sure her latest lover, the very cheesy Rudy, was at the Northgate Mall in Novato, projecting someone else's movie on a movie screen, followed by one of his frequent all-night "hanging out with the boys" thing. She made sure she had on hand a choice of any sort of liquor he could possibly want. For a new man, she dressed as I remember her dressing when I was young—very Tennessee Williams: something pink and frail and floating. She'd had her hair done; had long squared off nails glued over her gnawed fingertips.

Throwing myself on her flowered couch (yellow hibiscus against a mottled orange wash), I watched soaps while the two of them sat at her kitchen table and talked about Hollywood for hours. They also drank for hours. Always the actor, he played

William Powell playing Nick Charles. Greedy, if not needy, for men, she played a slightly off Blanche DuBois. As written, Blanche DuBois did not say "fuck" every few minutes.

Even starring in completely different movies, they got on pretty well. They both got drunk, she more than he. She spilled her drink on the Formica; he laughed. Her lipstick strayed onto her chin. One by one, the pins in her hair fell out. He laughed at that too. Said he'd buy her a wig, a hat, a make-over, whatever she wanted. She was pixilated with pleasure.

She embarrassed the hell out of me. She amused the hell out of him.

This is the last thing she ever said to me: "I've just had the most wonderful day of my life."

Mr. Honig is speaking. He's telling the wedding guests how happy he is they've come to share this wonderful day. The guests, Faye's neighbors, Faye's tradesmen, even the caterers, raise their glasses and drink to Mr. Honig's happiness. Mr. Honig is not a tall man and he's not short. He's not slender nor is he fat. His hair is neither black nor blond; his eyes neither brown nor blue. Mr. Honig is just a man, a very nice man with a yellow tie and a yellow rose in his buttonhole, toasting his new bride.

Faye feels a brief moment of warmth towards him in her own cold way.

It wasn't easy, but I climbed back into my room

by way of the fire escape.

This time I'm using a pen to write. I'm using paper. If I make a mistake I have an eraser. Short stories aren't my thing, but I find one flowing out on the page.

THE STAIRS IN THE BACK OF THE CLOSET

I pace. Occasionally I write a little something in my journal. I stand at my window and stare down into what one would imagine is a perfectly ordinary town. No matter how well appointed, I can't stay cooped up in this hotel room forever, but outside it seems close to a Biblical deluge. Who thought it could rain so much in Vermont, a region of lonely beauty, half-bewitched with tales of odd and curious lore? Certainly not myself, come all the way for this by tram and then by train from Miskatonic University in Arkham, Massachusetts. Indeed, I put aside all else I was doing and virtually raced to be here. For how could I, an instructor of literature and an enthusiastic amateur student of New England folklore, resist the strange and worrisome things being reported up here?

The day I arrived was cold and grey, but dry. I'd sat on the riverbank writing in my journal, inhaling all the smells of the thick green countryside, and then, I can hardly credit what I saw in the rushing grey water. Something floated by, something pink and bloated and unsightly. Something that made me decamp my spot immediately. It had waved at me. Not an arm, but a tentacle.

I've regretted leaving ever since. I should have stayed, should have made sure of what I'd seen.

But this rain, this veritable flood from the heavens, will not let up. For two days now I have been trapped in my room here in River House. Nor am I alone in my resistance to daring the great out of doors. From my window, I can see that no one else ventures out into the sad dark day. No one walks along Main Street in the incessant roaring wet, or shops in the drear and deserted stores, or even stands as I do looking out from behind their own dim windows. It's the rain. People have gotten sick of the rain. I imagine they're all in their beds, pillows over their heads to drown out the sound of the falling water. I am certain they ask themselves: when has there ever been a year like this year? When has there ever been this much rain?

From my room on the top floor of River House, I can see most of this rather quaint, rather charming, rather backward town. Emptying into the swollen Connecticut River, the Blackstone Brook is any minute now sure to burst its banks. Much more of this and it will flood Main Street, and then what shall this poor town do? Main Street is, as its name implies, the very spine of this small place. Should it flood, unthinkable woe would descend on all those who live here. For the moment though, the Blackstone rages between the ancient rocks that have contained it since time out of mind with a roar like an unending avalanche.

It's raining so hard, the rain bounces a foot back from the surface of the paved road below me. Less than a block away Island Park, and the bridge one needs use to get to it, squats in the middle of the great Connecticut River behind a thick grey curtain of rain. Closed for the season, the island is no more than hinted at. As for the much larger mass of mountain on the New Hampshire side, that does not exist at all. I can see the river though. It doesn't appear to be full of water; it seems more as if it flows with mercury or with molten lead, and the rain comes down so hard, it drills the shiny leaden surface with thousands and thousands of holes.

As I watch, my head pressed mournfully against the windowpane, the most magnificent river in New England rises by the hour. A huge branch floats by, spinning in the metallic water. I gasp as the whole of an enormous tree is washed downriver, parts of a pasture fence, an entire chicken coop, a single sodden chicken atop it.

It's what floats on the river that has brought me from my cozy room back in Arkham to River House in Little Sokoki, Vermont. It's what people have reported, shivering as they recall what they have seen, eyes half-mad with the memory...the very thing I saw my first day. But so briefly. How I curse myself for becoming alarmed, for leaving. I would see these things too, even if the sight of such horrors were to paralyze my rational mind, drive me beyond my ability to cope. But I am thwarted by the rain, by the terrible incessant, unendurable, unceasing rain.

Suddenly there is a tumultuous noise upriver, a tremendous crack! and then a shriek like an enormous nail being drawn out of an enormous board, and I turn and I see a wall of water running down the river, a wall taller than the island, taller than the sign that reads Island Park, almost as tall as the two-story dance pavilion, and I'm still watching as it smashes into the skater's shacks and in a split second the skater's shacks are nothing but kindling rushing across the island, submerging the racing track beside the pavilion, and I'm still watching as the wall of water reaches the grandstand, a dark green wall made of boards and bleachers and branches and boats and bats and bricks and doors and fish and—my god, I see them! I see the creatures. Torn away from their own secret and primordial places, exposed for all to see and to gasp at with horror, their hideous bodies sweep by, bodies that are as pink as boiled crabs and as bloated in death as rotted gourds. Each body has too many limbs, each limb has too many joints, each head, if it could be called a head, has too many eyes, each eye, if they be eyes, lacks a lid. There seem to be wings sprouting from backs; the wings seem made of naked membranous skin about which cling, even in roiling river foam, a thick coat of muculent slime. There seem to be antennae sprouting from "heads." And as they roll in the turbulence, they bring up first one morbid aspect of themselves, and then another. And another.

No matter the cost, I will leave this room, I will get as close to that boiling mass of outraged river as I possibly can, rain be damned, safety be damned. Nothing can stop me. I will haul one of those uncanny creatures from the greedy arms of the river, or die trying.

It's not a pencil...it's a knife. Not paper. It's the wall. Oh God, I've peed myself. Waking this time to find myself standing at my own window, I take one look at the wall, one look at the knife in my hand, and urine gushed down my legs.

The rain's stopped, clouds are drifting away. There are people in the streets below, lights coming on in windows above the shops, a blue moon rising.

I'm wearing his pajama bottoms, a tee shirt that says "New York Paris London Rome Little Sokoki," socks that don't say anything. They're just socks. My pajamas are soaked.

What have I been doing? I've been writing on the wall with a pencil, a marker pen, the tines of my fork, the tip of my knife. Here and there a word stands out, here and there a whole sentence, enough to understand that it's a story in trance, or an entranced story—but mostly it's gibberish. The wall is a shredded mess. Perhaps I could hide the hole in the closet, at least long enough to get away from River House, but this? An entire wall of sheetrock scrawled on, cut to ribbons?

I can't help myself. I burst into tears. I thought I understood torment. I thought I knew it. What could be more painful than the death of a child? But this, this is torment. I want it to stop. It must stop. What happens to me now? Along with all else, I'm channeling the guests of River House? Who have I just been? Someone created by Lovecraft? Lovecraft himself? My guess is Lovecraft himself on an off-day, one where his muse was under the bed hiding from the both of us. I am entirely certain I can't do this anymore. Just as Virginia Woolf knew when she had passed that marker in the psyche, one that stands rotting at the frontier of rational thought: "Beyond Here Lies... and Lies...and Lies." What is real? What is not real? How much that is not real is solid ground; how much is quicksand? Her suicide note to her husband read in part: "Dearest, I feel certain I am going mad again. I feel we can't go thru another of those terrible times. And I shan't recover this time. I begin to hear voices...I can't fight any longer...V."

Begin to hear voices, Virginia? I do not merely hear voices, I have become the voices. I become that which speaks. What am I becoming?

There is the slight possibility that I am not insane. But if that is so, then River House is as Hill House is. Shirley said nothing could exist under conditions of absolute reality. But what about the conditions I now endure—of absolute fantasy?

Is it because I killed him? Is it because I am a murderer? Excuse me. A murderess. Is it because I took his life and now I must take my own, but before I do, I must suffer the outrage of knowing I have no talent of my own, yet be filled with the talents of others? Am I slapping my own face, building my own purgatory word by word, image by image, hallucination by hallucination?

Who is the woman who, last seen, was a little girl?

I have to wash my pajamas. I have to wash myself.

It was two days past his forty-ninth birthday when he slipped in the kitchen, taking my sizzling sea bass with him. The layer cake I'd made him (black inside, white outside) was still untouched on the counter, the candles unlit. Above him, the wall over the stove was seriously on fire, flames leaping like brilliant orange monkeys from splattered wall to cabinets to shelves to curtains. A fourth of the kitchen was engulfed by fire when I turned from my chopping block, knife in hand. You only really need one good knife in a kitchen, and that knife is a chef's knife, preferably an all purpose eight inch high-carbon stainless steel model, forged if you're strong (they can weigh quite a bit), stamped if you're not. Mine was forged with a full tang. It's the balance that's important, how the knife feels in your hand. If the balance is right, you can do anything with a good knife: chop or pound or crush. If the blade is good and thick you can use a rocking motion for chopping, which was what I'd been doing when he took his naked tumble. And of course the blade must be thin at the tip as well as flexible so you can work around bones, and thick at the heel of the blade so that with one good whack you can chop through an entire chicken. Mine was, and still is, a Classic Wüsthof-Trident. You have to take care of a knife like that. It loses its edge fairly quickly (though not as quickly as the old fashioned carbon steel); its tip can easily chip. I kept mine sharp enough to shave with.

By the time I found myself looking down at him, he'd stopped screaming about his burnt arms and hands and thighs and his burnt crotch and was starting to scream about the fire rapidly engulfing our kitchen. "Help me up!" he was hollering as he slithered around in the hot oil spilt over the slick Spanish tiles, "And, goddammit, call the goddamn fire department. And the paramedics."

I remember what I was thinking. I was thinking if he wanted to get up, he could get himself up. I was thinking that our house burning down around us served us both right for Kate. I was thinking how ugly he looked down there on the fishy floor, how ugly the red marks on his white and hairy body, how ugly his face was with his mouth wide open and screaming like that. His famous movie star face so many people paid good money to see... what would they pay now to see his famous movie star crotch burnt red with fish fat?

And then he said, "Do something, you stupid cunt. You want to lose everything?"

And I think I said, but might only have thought, I've already lost everything. And so have you, you drunken asshole.

And then I walked the four steps it took to get to him from the butcher's block, and seeing me come, he held out his hand for me to grasp, so that I would help haul him away from the oil and the flames and the disaster that was his own drunken doing. By the light of a leaping kitchen fire, I leaned down—but rather than hold out my own hand, suddenly and for no reason I could understand at the time, with one good whack, I cut off his. The right hand. His best hand. As I've already said, a good chef's knife can do any job you ask of it, so long as it's taken care of, so long as it's regularly sharpened, so long as a cook has good knife skills. His entire hand came off at the wrist with satisfying ease, just like taking the drumstick off a turkey. I was not as surprised as he was. All you have to know is where the bones naturally connect. I'll bet it didn't even hurt him. Not with all the other pain he was feeling, not with the alcohol content of his blood, not with a blade as keen as mine. The hand skittered across the kitchen tiling like a hairless pink tarantula and wound up quivering under the Welsh dresser. We both watched its progress, watched it drain itself of blood: he with genuine incredulity, me with genuine interest.

Little time left now. It wouldn't be long before the fire was completely out of control. Already the ceiling over our heads was burning, sending down a crackling confetti of hot sparks that hissed when they hit the widening pool of movie star blood gushing from his wrist.

I bent to my work with a will I hadn't known in months. For Kate, I said. I said it over and over and over—for Kate.

If he said anything, and he did, right until the last deft flick of the knife, I don't remember a word of it.

"To Faye," he says, "to the health of Mrs. Honig." And as he speaks he and the wedding guests gather round Faye in her lawn chair, bunch up, squeeze in...and they all look down, their glasses in their hands. Faye is now in the exact center of a closed circle of happy neighborly faces, pleasant faces, peaceful people. It makes her tummy rumble.

Faye can see up their noses. Mr. Hunnicutt's nose is stuffed with stiff yellow hair. The young caterer's man with the ponytail has a large pimple in his. Faye twists her head round. She can't keep all their noses in sight at the same time, and she hates that... so she singles out Mr. Honig's nose, and stares up into that. Like the rest of Mr. Honig, there is nothing interesting inside his nose.

"To Faye," they all say in unison, holding their glasses high. But something is wrong here. Something is very wrong. The voices do not stop with her name. The voices go on and on and on—and the name they are speaking, the sound they are making, her name: Faye—

*is beginning to sound like Faaaazzzzzz. Does
sound like Faaaaazzzzz.*

*The wedding guests do not lower their
glasses. They do not drink. As a matter of
fact, there are no glasses.*

*There are no glasses. Or guests. Or
caterers. There is no Mr. Honig. Like the other
faces, like all the other faces, Mr. Honig's face
has run away like water down a drain. Eyes,
noses, mouths...gone. Faye understands.
Too late, she understands. She has made a
mistake. And the cost could be dear.*

Poor old Edna Ferber, ugly as a gall bladder
and ever dying with love for George S. Kaufman
who did not love her back, wrote somewhere: "Life
can't ever really defeat a writer who is in love with
writing, for life itself is a writer's lover until death—
fascinating, cruel, lavish, warm, cold, treacherous,
constant."

I can understand her passion for George.
How could you not love a man who could say,
"Ah, I see—forgotten, but not gone," to a man of
overweening self-regard who had been given a big
splashy 'Going-far-far-away from New York City
party', yet some weeks later steps out of a New York
City elevator George is stepping into? I too am half
in love with the writer of *The Man Who Came to
Dinner* and *You Can't Take It With You*. A man who
dared to write entire shows, with jokes, for the Marx
Brothers. For one thing, he made people laugh,
and for another he did not kill himself. But life
is constant, Edna? As in: always faithful? As in:
always there until it isn't there? Perhaps I missed

something when I read that. Perhaps something
was missing in me, like the part about being in
love with writing. I am not in love with writing.
I do it because it's all I know how to do. I do it
because I hide in it. I do it because in it I become
my characters, and am not required to be me, or at
least not the me I act out when I am not writing. I
do it because I feel safe doing it. My need to write
is more as Stephen King says of his writer "hero"
in *The Dark Half*: "He sometimes believed that the
compulsion to make fiction was no more than a
bulwark against confusion, maybe even insanity. It
was a desperate imposition of order by people able
to find that precious stuff only in their minds, never
in their hearts."

Was he right when he called me his Houdini
Heart? Am I a cold unfeeling bitch? Am I able to
wriggle my way out of anything?

Yes, I think he was right. I may not have begun
that way, not when I was young and awestruck
by tiny purple flowers hidden in the grass, by the
shape of roots in the deep woods, by the curve of
sweet water lured by the salt sea, by my own elfin
shadow on walls. But I've learned/earned/wormed
my way there by now.

This means I will get out of whatever mess I
am currently in here in River House. I will not
be netted and locked up for death-in-life in a
Retirement Home for the Criminally Insane. I
will die as I intend dying. Or even, maybe, live.
Somehow. But first I will climb those god-damned
stairs. Even if I can't climb the stairs without
somehow winding up in someone's book or movie or
short story, I will still stand in the tower and know

166

the heart of River House.

Just as I knew his heart. The one I keep with me always, perfectly pickled in its pickling jar. If I ever had real need, I could eat it out of my Houdini hand.

I've covered the scrawl on the wall by pinning up my blanket over it. To hide the three deep, closely placed, stab marks that my blanket can't reach, I've had to use my pillowcase. I've shut the closet door. Now I'm going outside for awhile. Breathe air that hasn't made its ragged way from end to end of the long stale corridors of River House, gone in and out of rooms not mine, in and out of lungs not mine. Nothing odd ever happens to me outside of River House, or at least, I don't think so. There was the dog with his beautiful boy on the river bank. Both boy and dog were certifiably odd when I surfaced from my plunge under the Connecticut River. There was the disappearance of the crane on Maple Street, and then its reappearance. There was the figure in the tower window I thought might be my mother and the woman who became a girl who is now a child when she walked the streets with the same dog. But all these things were and are as nothing compared to what goes on *in* River House.

This time, heart beating at warp speed, I'll go window shopping, perhaps have a cup of tea in Little Sokoki's rather homey tearoom. I could browse in a bookstore, see what's been published lately, what's selling, if anyone I know has a new book out, buy a postcard of Little Sokoki and send it...to whom? A long time ago I started feeling as Ingrid Bergman once felt. "I have time now for only two kinds of people," she said, "those who can make me laugh, and those who can further my career." He was the only person who could make me laugh. As for my career, my career has gone about as far as it's going to go. As a newly minted murderess, the only people who could further my latest career are the police, and they get plenty of postcards. The Zodiac Killer, the Son of Sam, lesser homicidal sociopaths, even Saucy Jack himself, all wrote to the cops. But these are serial killers, while I'm probably just your plain everyday one-person-only kind of killer. No urge to brag to the police. That leaves only me. Should I send myself a postcard?

Increasingly baggy jeans over his pajamas, sweater from the thrift shop over my "New York Paris London Rome Little Sokoki" tee shirt (also from the thrift shop), I'm off to be "normal" at least once more before I climb those now-you-see-me, now-you-don't stairs and really get to where they're going, no matter how I manage it. They probably go to the tower. And the way into the tower is obvious, of course, and has been ever since I saw the drawings on Benjamin Willow's walls. I have to break into the little house on the roof that once was home to the family of Charles River Akeley himself. I have to enter the vacant sixth floor of River House. And then I have to break back out of it, cross the roof, and do more breaking and entering into the south facing window of the tower.

That means I have to find more stairs. The ones that lead to the Akeley House.

If I were writing all this into a screenplay, it might not be a snap, but it would be doable for my intrepid heroine, with plenty of heart-stoppers

along the way. Little oh-my-god moments to keep
an audience on the edge of its seat. Since this isn't
a screenplay or a novel or even "real life"—real life
took a very wrong, very unreal, turn quite some
time back—I have no idea how the whole thing
will go. No script, no plans, no skills for such an
undertaking. Just me and what's left of my mind.
And, of course, my hammer. A hammer is always
useful. And my flashlight. Never forget that. I
don't suppose I'll need my knife, though I might
carry it anyway. Just in case. But I can't carry a
huge chef's knife in my pocket: I'll need a sheath.
Think a minute. If I take my flashlight and my
hammer, I'll need a—what? Well of course. How
obvious. I'll pop into the Little Sokoki hardware
store and buy a tool-belt. In one of his early
movies, not his best, though not his worst, he
wore a tool-belt, playing a psychotic undercover
cop posing as a carpenter. In that movie, he
was crazier than the villain, more dangerous by
half. Watching him ply his supposed trade, you'd
swear he could have built an entire barn single-
handed. You'd also actually swear he was truly
disturbed. Actually, he couldn't drive a nail. Or
a car. He went everywhere by taxi. Or by limo if
someone else paid for it. A tool-belt like his psycho-
carpenter-cop movie tool-belt would do just fine.

I'm sitting on a small dusty couch in Little
Sokoki's tearoom, a small place, easy to miss, even
easier to turn an ankle getting down to, tucked as
it is under an old brick building on the steep west
bank of the Connecticut. The couch faces the one
large window lit by fairy-lights and the window
faces the river, flowing by only yards away.

169

In front of the couch is a low table and on the table sits a cup of steaming tea. Plus a bun of some sort. I didn't order a bun. Under the table is a large paper bag with a brand new tool-belt in it; also fresh flashlight batteries, as well as a few little things that fit nicely in the tool-belt that I could not resist. (I learned as much, if not more, about carpentry from his role in that movie than he did.) Bugger the expense. What little money I have left is quite enough to last these last few days. My rent is paid to the end of the month and the end of the month will be without doubt the end of me.

Aside from the tea-maker, now gone back to hiding behind a bookcase where he can continue reading his book (nothing I'd write, or even read: an Anne Rice undead quasi-spiritual weirdly erotic rather heartless sort of thing), the place is empty of the warmth of other tea-drinkers, but otherwise charming. It's like the sitting room of someone with very little money yet still sweetly hopeful; someone who has aimed for quaint, but ended up with eccentric. There are fat chairs and thin chairs. Slightly shabby pillows and slightly knocked about stools. There are tall tables, standing like newborn foals on long and uncertain legs. There are short legged tables, not foals but full grown bulldogs, their broad backs swamped in magazines, mostly very old copies of National Geographic and Vermont Country Store catalogs. Hidden away somewhere, there's a cheap sound system playing New Age music: an unending loop of someone plucking a harp. It's the kind of plucky noise the beautiful but brainless Eloi would be listening to in H.G. Wells' *Time Machine*, while deep in the earth below them the brutal Morlocks would be gnawing on yet

another Eloi thigh bone at the same time banging
their thick heads together to early Black Sabbath.

Heaped on shelves are boxes and bags and
baskets of tea, every kind of tea. Interesting things
hang on the walls. Interesting things dangle from
the ceiling. The rugs underfoot are a bit bare, a
bit tattered. There are dead flies on the window
sills, in the corners of the room, under the bun and
pastry counter. There are two tired bees bumping
against the window doing what I'm doing: trying
to find a way out. Everything, including the teas,
is covered by a thin layer of dust. The tea itself is
terrible. Americans don't understand tea. It's all
too strong or too weak or not tea at all, but some
sort of berried citrus'd cinnamoned grassy brew
they think is healthy or invigorating or swimming
with antioxidants or whatever. I tried for a simple
cup of black Orange Pekoe, a little milk, a little
sugar. I got something that would eat my spoon if I
left it in too long. But I haven't come for the tea. I
have no intention of actually drinking the tea.

I've come to live out my last few ordinary hours
in an ordinary fashion.

Of course it doesn't work out that way. Nothing
has ever been ordinary in Little Sokoki, Vermont,
at least not for me. The beautiful young man, last
seen at my door holding out an innocent apple (but
now, as I recall the moment, it seems more as if I
were Snow White and he a wicked queen—or maybe
it was the other way round), has just walked into
the tearoom. He sees me immediately. How could
he miss when I am the only customer here?

"Ah," he says, seating himself on my small
couch, without invitation or encouragement, "I've
been looking for you."

171

Looking for me? Why? He wants to give me another apple? Or he wants to converse? I don't do conversations anymore. I'm out of practice, out of patience, and out of time in several more ways than one. (Although I used to write great dialogue. A director or a producer wanted to perk up his picture with a little wit, a little classy Tracy-Hepburn give and take, he or she came to me. But all that is, like everything else, gone now.)

I say nothing, but this seems better than nothing to him. He signals the tea-maker from his book. "Lapsa Oolong, please." And then turns his attention to me.

I must look a sight. Days and nights and days of adventures in relative reality, the body neglected, the mouth turned down, the eyes turned inward, the soul readying itself for a leap into a void, any void. Does he see all this? Oh crap. He still has his camcorder. It's in a small black bag, the bag is zipped shut, but I know he has it. I know he wants to use it. On me. To record what he sees in me. Dissolution? Despair? Corruption? Even so, how beautiful this one is. I am used to beautiful people. In our world, we were surrounded by them. In his own way, he was beautiful. In my own way, I was beautiful. Every year, much of America's beauty: young, clueless, vain, desperate for fame, needy, and aside from the excessive quality of greed, quite ordinary, makes the trek to New York or to Hollywood. Once gathered in one spot, they all become somehow...less. Less unusual, less beautiful, less confident, though no less greedy. But no matter how much less they become, en masse they make the rest of us look worse than we already do. No fat, no bad teeth, no bandy legs or bulbous noses or sticky-out ears or acne scars. No cripples, no malformed, no diseased—on the outside.

But here in Little Sokoki, all alone amidst the usual assortment of the plain, the ordinary and the downright ugly, this young man shines like an angel.

I don't ask why he's been looking for me. I spend no more than a moment remembering I once thought to look for him...as a partner or a helper or at least a sympathetic ear. I don't drink my tea or eat my unordered bun. I merely sit on my couch, my last hope for a last taste of normal life gone. All I'm doing now is waiting him out.

His tea delivered and steaming beside him, he leans close. "I know who you are."

I think: that's more than I know. But it jolts me. I admit it moves me. Not that I show it. I am immobile. I seem impassive. I say, "Who am I?"

"A writer."

If I were to be drawn out, if he could accomplish that, I would now say, "I was." And he would either say, "You still are," or, "What makes you say that?" Either way, we'd be off, we'd be having a conversation, and somewhere along the way he'd want to take out his camcorder and film me, a real writer in a small town without doubt filled with writers as every town and every city all over the world are filled with writers. We are Legion. Most of us think there's a story in us. Some of us think the story we're full of is important enough to share with others. And we all begin with the same pathetic dream. To write something that will make other people love us. And when they do, we can then pretend, like Mailer, like Salinger, like

Thomas Pynchon, like Dorothy Parker, like Hunter
S. Thompson, like Capote, like Hemingway, like,
like, like…to scorn them for having been duped—
because no writer feels good enough to be loved.
Except, maybe, bad writers.

One of the best things Hunter ever said was:
"Real writers are monsters." I am again defined.
I may not be a good writer but I am a real writer
which means I am a monster.

"You wrote *The Windigo's Daughter.*"

Oh, fuck.

"There was a movie made out of it." Smiling,
he sips his Lapsa Oolong, the smell of which,
combined with the incessant plucking harp music,
makes me slightly ill. But since I am already
sickened by his naming my most famous book,
it hardly matters. "Of course," says he, "the
movie wasn't a patch on the book. The book was
fantastic. But that's normal, isn't it?"

Normal? I have no idea anymore what's
normal. I only know one thing for certain. He isn't.
There's something about him that's very abnormal.
What is it? The smile? The beauty? The apple?
The fact he lives in River House and River House
is not for the usual run of the mill hominoid?
This conversation? He knows what I've written.
Therefore he must know who I was married to, who
I am the recent widow of. I repeat: oh fuck.

Now we both sit quietly. He's working hard
here, holding his breath, maintaining his cool,
sipping his tea. Me, I'm watching mine grow cold,
eying my bun and idly imagining the life forms
it supports, even now, before it begins to decay.
This bun will end up out back of the tearoom in a
garbage can. I think of who will fish it out again, of

who will eat it, rot and all.

I am about to heave. I am also just about to get up and leave, when he says, "Did it begin as an accident?"

I know exactly what he's talking about. He's asking if I flensed, filleted, sliced and chopped him up into rather small pieces by accident. He wants to know what I did with his head. It's in the news. No head. He wants to know if the fire was an accident. I think: if he thinks any of the above was no accident, he's taking a big risk confronting a murderess, now isn't he? I've seen movies that contain a scene like this. Lots of them. Too many. Some heedless fathead who can't imagine being killed by someone who has killed before, dying to have answers to what might be his dying questions. This variation of the "idiot in the attic" wants to know what it was like to murder someone, particularly what it was like to kill a movie star. As written by me and most everyone else, the typical idiot hardly ever achieves his desire to feel what the killer felt (ah, but there *was* Kevin Costner's *Mr. Brooks*, wasn't there? damn good movie, but again a case in point), but he does get to know how the victim felt. I was right. This one is not normal. Or maybe he is. People are monkeys and monkeys are such a curious bunch.

His fingers are touching his camcorder case, a slight caress. I see he wants to film me answering his questions. He thinks it will make him famous. The man, the youth, who caught the notorious Hollywood screenwriter and novelist who murdered one of the world's greatest stars.

For the first time I really look at him. He's looking at me, his blue eyes all bogus seeing, all bogus knowing, all cod pity, all ultimate greed...and all completely stupid.

I have little choice. He's just taken it from me. I may not want to live much longer, but I sure as hell don't want this little beauty turning me in, living off my name, not to mention his name, for the rest of his life. But most of all, most importantly of all, I will not have him trading in on Kate's death.

I really don't want to. It's the truth. I swear it. I swear on my daughter's grave, I honestly hate having to do what I must do.

But, at least, it ought to be easy. All I have to do is invite him back to my room in River House and, well, basically—kill him.

And even though he has everything to lose, he'll come. Dumb fuck is living breathing prey. He thinks he's a predator, but he's dead meat. Me, all along I've thought myself a hero. Not a great hero, not one to remember, but nevertheless heroic. But now, by doing what he's forcing me to do, I will also become the villain. Which, storywise, is a good thing. There is no story without conflict. No story can exist without a villain.

I am what I am. I do what I do. Villains are always the hero in their own story. Villains always have a reason for what villainy they get up to. Me, I just need a little more time. A little more time is all I ask for. This beautiful boy is the villain to my hero; he's going to take my time away from me. He's going to make a spectacle of my life, and of Kate's. He's going to require me to continue living, a captive subject of endless chatter and patter and pity and horror and scorn. In order to further himself, he will condemn me to the tabloids, to the law, and to my own ongoing conscious awareness.

To do nothing about it is to be neither hero nor villain. To do nothing is the coward's choice, a choice made by most people for the whole of their lives. I am a choice-maker. I am now making my choice. I will be the villain to his hero as he is villain to mine. I will not let him have his way.

As I gather my things, as he pays for everything, including my unordered uneaten bun, I speak to him. I say, "The day I first saw you, outside the Brooks House...was that your dog?"

He looks at me, definitely guileless, opened by surprise. "What dog?"

Here's a little more of the book he remembers so well, the one he thinks is better as a book than a movie.

What was once Mr. Honig is now a very big bee wearing a yellow tie, but the yellow of the tie blends with the yellow of his bee fur. And what once were wedding guests are now a swarm of bees. Very big bees, bees as big as wrens. All the bees, including the bee Faye has just married, are buzzing and buzzing and fanning their enormous wings which lifts them from the lawn like flies, or like hummingbirds, or like tiny helicopters. Like helicopters, their wings push at the air, turn it into wind, and the wind flattens the skin of Faye's keening face.

If she only had her slingshot.

Baring her teeth, Faye snaps at the bees. For the first time ever, although Faye has always known how to cause fear, she now knows how to feel fear. She knows what fear means. For Faye, it means shrieking up out of her chair, it means throwing the skirt of her bloodred dress over her head, it means screaming and screaming and running around the table on her back lawn windmilling her arms like a woman chased by bees.

If you are a presentable and seemingly willing female, it's easy to get a heterosexual male to do almost anything. So easy, even now when I am far from my best it feels a little like cheating. But then I remember why he's come, and I know he's thinking the same thing. How easy it is for someone with his beauty to get a female to do almost anything. Especially an older female who's in a world of trouble.

Whatever.

Here he is in my chevron of a room in River House, already counting his coins, already imagining what he will say to the world's press when they ask him how he knew it was me, how I looked, acted, what I said. He's already visualizing his tape of my confessing to him appearing on YouTube, as well as on every news show, in every tabloid, on every chat show in the U.S., if not the world. After all, I killed the man who will probably win a second, albeit posthumous, Oscar for *Cheat the Devil*. I'm the woman who hid his head. They'll ask him how he captured me. I can tell he'll be humble. He'll act his heart out. Come to think, I'll bet he intends to parlay this whole thing into a Hollywood contract.

Damn. If I were still writing, I'd use all this. I

honestly think it might make an interesting little movie. With a premise like this premise, with a great hook in the first killing, and then a second great hook in a second killing, I would probably be allowed to direct the thing. That is, if I could do it from Death Row.

If I wrote this as a movie, I'd leave out River House. River House doesn't have a beginning or an end and it has one hellish mess of a second act. River House doesn't make any kind of story sense. Can't use it. Can only live it.

In any case, so far, I've said very little. To his question, "Did it begin as an accident?" I answered in almost a whisper, "I'll show you." And then I got up, retrieved my brown paper bag from under the table, and left the tearoom. Just as I thought he would, the fool followed me.

What do I care if the tea-maker with his nose still in his book of Rice saw us leave together? What do I care if anywhere along Main Street, or in the corridors of River House on our way up to the third floor, someone else took note of our passing? What was going to happen was so much more for Kate than for me. What was going to happen would happen whether I got caught or not. But I won't get caught. Not by the living.

As I walked, as he walked beside me, I thought: there was a time I assumed suicide was my limit... that is, if I could ever work up the nerve. Now, after the carnage in my kitchen, after the fire, after the night in a Motel 6, after River House and whatever River House is, after this unhappy, but unavoidable, decision, I know I don't know my limits. It's possible I have no limits. It's possible no one has limits save those imposed by fear: fear of God, fear of others, but stronger than these, fear of self.

The mood I'm in, I find that almost interesting.

Hollywood has ever been awash with gorgeous gays playing it straight. They have to—leading men are straight men, and that's that. Seen on film, though some might suspect, most people never really know. Cary Grant got away with it; Rock Hudson did pretty well...and those he and I knew are still doing fine. (A real regret: that I won't be seeing any of them, ever again. Gays are my favorite sex.) Pretty as he is, this one is straight, I'm sure of it. If he weren't, I'd still be playing him along, but I'd play him differently.

Since he's straight, I've decided to pretend I'll fuck him. Or perhaps, being that much older than he is, I might have to pretend I'm anxious that he fuck me. Whichever...cleaned up and sober, I'm still attractive; the prospect of sex for whatever reason is the only surefire way to get him not only into my bathroom, but into my shower.

When the fire consumed our kitchen, when I cut him up into pieces to the sound of screaming and sizzling blood, it was all done on the spur of the moment, nothing planned, nothing premeditated. This time I'm premeditating like mad. I'm watching, though I don't seem to, every movement my would-be betrayer makes, every movement I make. I'm calculating what to do if he doesn't do what I want him to do. What to do if he does. Now that he's here, it's become obvious he thinks he'll allow me, Mrs. Movie Star Murderer, to seduce him. He thinks I'll be so weak and so bleak and so remorseful that later, after being thoroughly serviced by beauty, I'll lie in bed, naked and sated and grateful and saddened, and let him film my confession.

Shit. He's staring at my room. His room must be similar, but in mine there's nothing but a bed which is a futon on the thinning brown carpet. There's one small lamp. There's one small traveling clock. There's a laptop by the lamp. There's the large brown paper bag that I've just carried in. There's me. There's him. That's it. And on the futon only one sheet, not dirty but none too clean, one pillow, no pillowcase, no blanket. He's looking for my blanket. He's probably also looking for my pillowcase. Ah, there they are, pinned to the wall next to the window. He's curious to know why I pinned my pillowcase and blanket to the wall. He's more than curious. He's a bit anxious about it. This is tricky. I can't spook him, not yet anyway. If he sees what's all over the wall under the blanket and pillowcase, I might lose him. He'll bolt. If I were him, I'd bolt. I can't let that happen. I really can't allow him to leave this room.

He wants me. He urgently wants what he thinks I can give him: fame, money, open doors, so he certainly doesn't want to leave, but exactly how big are his balls? He thinks he's alone in a room with a killer. Being alone in a room with your ordinary everyday driven-to-do-it husband killer is one thing, but being alone with a possible completely freaked out psycho killer is another thing.

Time for a quick diversion. A woman stripping is always diverting. A woman stripping and talking dirty at the same time is even more diverting. I've used it in more than one screenplay.

It works of course, just as it does in the movies.
Men. Such easy prey. Which is why so many men
hate women...or at least fear them, which is much
the same thing. They know, even if they don't know
they know, that a smart good-looking woman holds
all the cards. They know, even if they don't know
they know, that males are the weaker sex. Why
else would they repress females all over the world
from the dawn of historical time?

I'm slowly peeling off my clothes, telling him
what I want him to do to me, telling him how much
I'm going to like it, how much he's going to like it...
and yes, there he goes, he's losing it. Temporarily
losing his need for fame and glory, losing his
fear of whatever my blanket and pillowcase
mean. Another, stronger, need is taking over.
His breathing has changed. His face is getting
red. His Newman blue eyes are glazing over. He's
already dropped his camcorder case on the floor
by the foot of my futon. He's slipped off his jacket.
He's working on his shirt buttons. By the time
I'm stepping out of my panties, he's unzipping
his pants. He's ready. He's *too* ready. If I'm not
careful, he'll be on me like a dog on a bitch, and
then I'll have to think of a new game. I don't want
to think of a new game. This is my game. So I
say, "You know what turns me on the most? It's
a man who's clean...really clean." And I point at
my bathroom. In which there's a shower. And a
shower curtain.

Oh sweet. He's shy. He shuts the bathroom
door to take his shower. Which is perfectly fine by
me. I'm naked now. Not a stitch on. I can hear
him in there, water hitting his fine hard body, water
hissing down the drain. I may have five minutes,

I might only have two. No messing around. No longer completely unclothed, I'm now wearing the new tool-belt like a gunslinger wears his gunbelt. Open the closet door, find the hammer, drop it through a loop on my left hip. Find the chef's knife. Slip that into a handy leather loop slung from my right hip. The other stuff I bought in the Little Sokoki hardware store can wait. Right now, I've got all I need. Except a grey wig, a shapeless housedress, a thick pair of baggy support hose, and some down-at-heel old lady shoes. But personally, this is my movie, not Hitchcock's. I'm going in as myself.

Slowly, half-inch by half-inch, opening the bathroom door, seeing his shape busy lathering up behind my should-be white shower curtain, drawing my knife from its loop, I find I'm not nervous. I'm not nervous at all. Why is that, I wonder? Is it because I've done this before? Is it because I'm good at it? Is it because I like doing it? No time to worry about such things now. Work to do here.

His heart is not mine. I let him keep it.

Such a busy day. Not even a cup of tea to sustain me.

I unpin my blanket from the wall, hardly notice the Lovecraftian slice and scrawl, crawl into bed for a nap. Leave the pillowcase. Don't need a pillowcase. I've still so much to do, but first a nap. Killing is very tiring. I really need a little nap.

I awake in total darkness. Fumble around for the lamp switch. What time is it? How long have I slept? Clock says 9:45 P.M. The sounds of Little

Sokoki at night drift up to my window. Shouting
and laughter from the patrons of *The Last Ditch*. A
slight rain still falls, causing passing cars to whisk
whisk *whisk* by. Comes a distant truck horn out
on the Interstate. The sound of my own breathing
is heavy in my ears. The sound of my heart is
heavier.

I crawl to the fridge, pull myself up by its
handle.

There's a knife in the sink; there's a hammer
on the drain board, both washed clean. There's a
tool-belt on the floor in front of the bathroom door.
There's a camcorder in its case on the floor near the
closet. There's two bottles in the fridge. One red
wine and one white wine. I've had enough red for
awhile. White wine is fine.

I crawl back to drink the white in bed.

I'm not crazy. I know there's a dead man in my
bathtub. But I'm not Norman Bates and this isn't
the Bates Motel. No car, no body bundled into the
trunk, no driving to a deserted pond and sinking
the victim's car deep into the muck. No walking
back to the motel and pretending my mother did it.
My poor mother would kill herself before she'd kill
someone else.

It occurs to me...all I did was reverse the
process.

I've cleaned myself, but I'm not cleaning up the
mess in the bathroom; I haven't the time to waste.
If I need to wash anything again, including me, I'll
wash in the kitchen sink. If I need to pee, I'll pee in
the kitchen sink. If I have a greater need, I'll brave
the bathroom. I seldom have greater needs on a
diet of seeds and a little cheese.

Thinking of the body in the bathroom reminds

me of Dennis Nielsen again. I could find acid. How many bodies have been gotten rid of by reducing them to tallow with acid? But I have no interest in getting rid of the body. Finally caught, Dennis told the revolted police, "No one ever wants to believe that I am just an ordinary man come to an extraordinary and overwhelming conclusion."

What an interesting observation. I'd like to think the same of myself; just an ordinary woman driven by circumstance to extraordinary lengths. I'd like to, but I can't. No killer is ordinary, not even Dennis with his exceptional insight and strange honesty. No artist is ordinary. No writer is ordinary. No mystic is ordinary. No one who's haunted is ordinary. "Ordinary" doesn't do anything or feel anything or think anything that lifts her or him or it above the teeming mass of humanity. Or sinks them below it. Simple as that.

When I say things like this to ordinary people, they're forever getting furious, and almost always because they suspect they're ordinary.

Too bad. Too sad. Too true. They *are* ordinary.

I really am sorry the poor thing had to wind up in my bathtub. I'm sorry he saw me as a great opportunity. I'm sorry he saw me at all. I'm sorry. I'm sorry. For all of us. All over the world, ordinary or not, we live lives of pain and waste—and will, each and every one of us, sooner or later become a feast for ordinary flies.

On the other hand, never waste a promising story. And what an unlikely arc my life has taken on; perfect for the movie business which cranks out unlikely stories like Michael Crichton used to crank out great hooks and bad writing. (I'd bet anything

Crichton never had a single suicidal moment.)
Laptop back in my lap, boot it up, open a blank
Word file. Don't bother to format. Write.

SYNOPSIS

Perhaps I can get at least an outline on the
page before he starts to stink, or even more than
an outline. Hasn't King been known to produce
a hundred thousand words in less than a week?
Am I exaggerating? Does King? But after all, as
William Faulkner said: "Everything goes by the
board: honor, pride, decency...to get the book
written. If a writer has to rob his mother, he will
not hesitate; the *Ode on a Grecian Urn* is worth any
number of old ladies."

Or in this case, any number of young and
ambitious males. Trouble is, I couldn't write
something like *Ode on a Grecian Urn* to save my life.
Question is: would I want to? Save my life? Oh,
no. But write like Keats? Oh, yes.

> *"...Beauty is truth, truth beauty—that is all*
> *Ye know on earth, and all ye need to know."*

I wake with a jump start at 12:24 A.M. Fell
asleep again, right in the middle of a sentence.
But I did it. I got the basic premise written. It's
all there, still on my screen. For some reason,
whatever's erased every single thing I've tried to
write since coming to River House has left this final
thing.

So there, I've managed a legacy, something to
leave behind. And I have had my last "normal"
day. I would laugh, but somehow laughter

seems unseemly when there's a fresh kill in your
bathroom. Will he in his turn haunt River House?
Or does it retain only the impressions of the artists
who've passed through? Seems to me River House
could do with a real ghost, one who violently died
here, one who no doubt hoped to star in Hollywood.
In River House he can play the lead in some first
rate material. (Oh. Not nice. Not nice at all. I
seem to be getting meaner the longer I allow myself
to live. Not good to be so bad. Must stop.)

It's time now to do as I've intended doing all
along. Or been pointed towards all along—if not
by me, then by some aspect of me. And if not by
me or some aspect of me, then by someone in River
House, or something in River House. Or perhaps,
like Hill House, River House itself. It really doesn't
matter which of these urges me towards my fate.
What matters is the implacable urge. By hook or
by crook, by the stairs in the back of my closet
or by breaking into the "sixth floor" house on the
roof, I will get into the tower. I don't know why I
know what I know, but I am certain that the tower
holds my answer. It's the end of everything. Or
the beginning of nothing. Either way is fine by me.
When I first arrived in Little Sokoki I said I had
nothing left to lose. Now I have even less. I have
nothing left to gain. When it's all over, my literary
executor who is also my agent will eventually find
this file on my laptop. She'll hire a writer, a good
writer, one who can actually make something of it,
attach a star to play me and one to play him, and
at that point someone briefly "important" in some
production company or other is certain to give it a
green light. In the credits there'll be a card reading:
"Based on a true story." As for my posthumous

writer's credit, that will say: from an idea by...
Or maybe not.

In two hours it will be 3 A.M. Three in the
morning is reality's weakest moment, the time
when other worlds and other beings have their best
shot at entering our world. And vice versa. And
I am in Vermont. Vermont—the place Lovecraft
called bewitched, that Hitchcock filmed as a fantasy
of easy death, where the washed-up silent movie
icon Louise Brooks came to die just like me, but
wound up writing books instead (not that it did
her much good), the land in which Shirley Jackson
chose to live out her strange and uneasy life. In
The Windigo's Daughter I wrote: "*Tonight she will
be somewhere else: upper New York State perhaps,
or by the shores of what she's heard is the fogblue
water of a great salt sea. Wherever she is, there will
be magic still, just as there is magic everywhere, but
not like Vermont's magic. Away from a place like
Vermont, the heart grows fainter, the spells weaker,
the call dimmer, the beat slower. Outside is less
primordial, more obvious. It's shabbier, trickier. It's
just what Faye is looking for.*"
I am not my hungry heroine Faye; I have
discovered strong magic is just what I have been
looking for. It's what I once found, and then lost,
long ago when I was still a child. But I have to find
it again by 3 A.M.
Oh hell. I must correct myself. I am not only
hungry, I'm famished. I'm so hungry I double over
with stomach pain. I haven't eaten since, since...I
have no idea when I last ate whatever it was I
last ate. So painful: suicide by starvation must
be almost as bad as suicide by lye. But there's

nothing to eat, not in my ugly little pantry, not in my refrigerator, not in my room. Oh, silly me. But of course there's something to eat. Something I brought with me, something that's been here all along. It's in my leather bag. Aren't all condemned prisoners allowed a last meal?

Besides, all along, like Dante, it's been my intention to "... eat that burning heart out of his hand."

Or, in this case, *my* hand.

I'm all in black except for my leather tool-belt which is the color of very old oatmeal. I wish it too were black, but the hardware store doesn't carry black tool-belts. In it I've found room for all sorts of things: hammer, chef's knife, flashlight, nail sets (I know I'll be opening things, but you never know what I might be closing), hand powered brace and bit with a phone man's drill, a sheetrock handsaw, wire cutters, a picture framer's glass cutter, a Stanley knife, the camcorder, a cheap watch because time will be important, my room key (I've checked and triple-checked, the door to my room is locked; imagine the scene if someone were to mistake my room for their own very similar room, walk on in, and need a shower), a bottle of red wine with corkscrew (I thought of bringing a wineglass, but why look silly?), a cunning little flexible laser pointer, and a sealed jar full of something I've carried all the way from California. I'm wearing a black woolen cap on my head and my black tennis shoes on my feet. A cat burglar couldn't be better, or more oddly, dressed. I'm not using my stairs. For one thing, at the moment, they're not there. Nothing is there but a messy ceiling-tile covered hole in the back wall of my closet.

For another, no matter if they were there: narrow or wide or circular, they'd only lead to ideas not mine, to brilliant work already done by someone else. So what I'm doing is avoiding the noise made by the elevator (and also avoiding, I admit, that she might be in it, with her dog: she younger, he smaller, darker and bloodier), and climbing instead a "real" staircase, the one that leads from the ground floor lobby all the way up to the fifth floor. Once on the fifth floor, I will avoid the room with the apple outside the door and find a way to the house on the roof. There must be a way and it must be obvious. It was, after all, the entrance to the home of Charles River Akeley & family.

Charles was born right here in Little Sokoki, and he died right here in Little Sokoki. I don't know much about him. I know I should have learned more (a wife? Two wives? Three? Children, yes or no? Habits? Character? Died when? Died how? Any scandals, good deeds, mysteries?), after all I'm a writer, and any writer worth her salt does research. But it's too late now.

He, I learned a great deal about. Born as far as one could get from someplace like Vermont, to wit: El Paso, Texas—dry, dirty, hot, and on the road from nothing to nowhere. I know he was the son of an irrigation pump salesman. I know his hard-worked used-up mother died giving birth to him, that he came into the world with no mother, but did have a nine year old sister. He and his sister must have had one hell of a dad though, because the man did not remarry, did not fob the kids off on some other woman, did not have more

children to prove his manliness. He did not drink, raise hell, fuck whores, drive fast, or spend all his money on himself in one stupid way or another. On the other hand, he had no humor and no imagination, although I suppose it took some sort of imaginative process to believe so firmly in Hell, even if the Hell he believed in was the product of other men's morbid idiot fancy. He also believed that virtually every human on earth was bound to wind up in that Hell, except himself, and by God, his goddamned kids.

In grim silence, he raised his motherless daughter and his motherless son all by himself. He paid for their Catholic schooling. More to his credit than theirs, they both managed to get through their teenage years without too much trouble. He sent them to Catholic colleges (if they hadn't chosen Catholic, he wasn't paying), attended their graduations, lived alone, never stopped working the same job, then died of a massive coronary a few years before either one of them made it good.

The sister moved away from El Paso to study religion at a college in Dallas, but with Dad no longer breathing brimstone over her shoulder, turned instead to painting. It took her a long time, even when her brother blossomed into a Hollywood star, but she's become very well regarded in the Southwest, paints the heat and dirt of Texas like a smaller more precise Georgia O'Keefe. Four of her canvases burnt along with the Malibu house. I regret that immensely. I regret not being able to tell her I'm sorry. (But then I remember that all his money, and all of mine come to think, will be hers soon enough. She's going to be able to buy a lot of paint.) As for him, he came out to California

to play baseball for Loyola Marymount University
in Los Angeles. Not too long after that, he began
appearing around L.A. in any play, large or small,
good or bad, anyone would cast him in. He said
he did it because it got him laid. I believe that. He
certainly got laid. Sex wasn't one of his hang-ups:
sometimes he got laid to get the part and sometimes
it was a woman and sometimes it wasn't. As an
actor, when he was good, he was very very good,
a rumpled Bogie, a half brother to Mitchum, a full
brother to Nolte. When he wasn't all that good, it
was almost always the play, sometimes the director,
and later, often the drink. He was hardly ever bad.
Even drunk, he had that magic. He could turn in a
performance.

It took him about a year to be tapped for the
silver screen, another two years to become a major
star. It took him five to become a major drunk.

Unlike some leading men, he liked to talk in
his pictures, the more blather the better. He was
always looking for great dialogue. He said that's
why he took the role in my movie. He got to say
clever things, insightful, funny things. Later, lying
on his back on the rocky sand under the pilings
that held his Malibu house above the tossing sea,
he said, "The movie business is a crock of shit."

I said, "Is that why you drink?"

For that, he gave me one of those ten-million-
dollars-a-picture-plus-a-percentage looks, and
said, "I'm not my Dad. I don't even wish I was, the
miserable fuck. Not drinking killed him. Hell, I'd
fucking drink if I sold irrigation pumps all my life.
I'd fucking drink if I had two little kids looking to
me for everything they ever needed. I'd fucking
drink if one of my kids painted virgin Catholic

pussy. I'd fucking drink if the other never became a priest—that's what he wanted. Wanted me to be a gardener for God planting demons in little kid's souls. Hell, you think I drink because I'm an actor making an ass of myself every single day of my life, which I do and which I am?"

I didn't have a clue why he drank. I didn't have a clue, period. I barely knew him. But then, at this point, he wasn't really talking to me.

"I drink because one of those demons came up like a fucking tulip, a black raging demon that hates my guts and that never gets tired of telling me about it. Fucking thing's talking to me now, it'll be talking to me an hour from now. It'll be the last voice I ever hear. I wake up with it and I go to sleep with it. It drives me to rage and it drives me to panic and it drives me to despair and it just fucking drives me, period. Only three things touch it, and I've tried everything, believe me, every stupid kind of messed-up crap a man can do to himself."

Silence then, until I asked, "Three things?"

"Drink, fuck—or pretend I'm someone else."

I heard this, I heard it clearly, and I still sat there on the stinking sand under his house, still went up to his bedroom a while later.

We were made for each other. Kate never had a chance.

But here's a thought to make me smile. There were four things that could shut up that voice. Death was that fourth thing. He should thank me.

Walking the fifth floor corridors of River House in the middle of the night is no different than walking any other corridor on any other floor of River House: the same dark doors to the same

efficiency apartments, the same exit signs, the
same soiled carpeting, the same drab paint, the
same dim recessed neon lighting. No windows
because the windows of River House are in the
apartments. Of course, like the second floor, the
fifth has an apartment I hope never to see again.
5-4, the one with the apple lying on the tatty carpet
outside its door, the one I thought was the boy's
apartment and might actually, for all I know, *be* his
apartment. No apple now. And no girl with a fist of
steel to drag me in, not if I don't knock on the door.

Besides this, the ballroom is on the fifth floor.
I've quickly checked both wings, High Street and
Main Street. If there was once a door up here, an
entrance to a private staircase for the Akeley family,
it's gone now. There isn't even space for what
must once have been in River House, the Akeley's
access to their little home on the roof. I can think
of only one solution to this puzzle because there
is only one place left to look. The entrance has to
have been through the ballroom. This was Charles
River Akeley's building. He had it built to his
personal design and he paid for it with the riches
he took from the men who ripped the gold from the
California earth. If he had a reason for putting the
staircase to his own home in the ballroom, I can't
imagine what it was. Or maybe I can.

Perhaps the ballroom came much later.
Perhaps before it was a ballroom, the space served
as a grand entrance to Akeley's conceit of a house
on the roof of his nose-thumbing building. Or
perhaps the ballroom was the lower part of his
private home, divided into things like his living
room and kitchen and dining room and such, and
perhaps in later years, he retreated to the small

195

roof house for some reason, allowing what was once part of his personal apartments to become a ballroom. I don't know. All I know is that I've already been in the ballroom, now nothing more than a huge storage room full of junk and ancient cast-offs, looking for a way into the tower. I can't even recall how long ago that must have been; life before River House dims, even life in River House fades as it passes but it seems I have lived here for a long long time, so long life before River House no longer exists, therefore—what has it to do with me? (Aha. An interesting defense strategy. If I were still a writer, I could use that in a TV courtroom drama.) Whenever it was I was last here, I found no staircase up to the largest tower above me, no extension of the stairs that come and go in my closet.

Once again, I stand in front of the ballroom's double glass doors. Unlike the first time, they're locked; even bad maintenance men can get it right from time to time. Good thing the doors are made of glass and that I've brought a specialized glass cutter. Good thing I've regained my sanity on this day of all days. I now define sanity as the ability to function as if reality were real. In any case, I can actually work the glass cutter, and do it with very little noise. These good things come from watching movies and learning what tools to carry and what to do with them. First, near the doorknob, place a chromium-plated handle over the glass. Second, superglue the thing by its flat metal discs to the glass and wait about a second for the glue to dry. Third, cut a hole around the handle with the diamond cutting edge big enough for my hand and forearm, keeping hold of the circle of glass with the superglued handle so that it doesn't fall and shatter on the floor. Then, gently but firmly, tap out the glass, and when that's done, slip my hand through and unlatch the door. Simple. And finally—walk in. Naturally it isn't as easy as that. The glass is as thick as a coffee table top. For a moment there, I'm sure that the pressure I have to apply to "tap out the glass" is going to shatter the whole door. Thank someone, it doesn't.

Can't use my flashlight for the same reason I couldn't use it in Benjamin's office, whenever that was. There must be a cop out there somewhere. But enough light comes through the twelve foot tall windows from the streetlamps to make things visible. I can see just enough to get around without bumping into things, but I admit it's a little bit spooky...which makes me smile in the pale light. To anyone else but me, I am the spooky one. I am the bad one.

It takes only a glance to see that the corner tower is quite a distance from Akeley's roof house; essentially, the entire length of the ballroom. My first time here, I never looked other than under the tower. Very obviously the way up to the Akeley's house has to be under Akeley's house.

But first I'll have to move about twenty old sinks, half as many old toilets, and a small mountain of cheap furniture.

I'm already tired. It's dimmer, darker, less comforting so far from the windows, and picking up and moving toilets as well as dismantling a furniture mountain (as quietly as an elf; don't want to be caught here at this hour, at any hour), has taken most of the energy I began this with. I rest on an overturned toilet bowl, look out one of the ballroom's huge windows. The little watch I bought reads one thirty-five in the morning. Little Sokoki seems to be in bed early tonight, even the guests of *The Last Ditch.* The streets are empty. No sound of a car or a motorcycle anywhere, no distant movement on the Interstate. No late night drunks falling about, no disillusioned kids lurking in shadows selling each other drugs, no dwellers in cardboard out scrounging for snacks in the dumpsters. There are no lights in any of the windows, not even in one of the private houses on the hills rising to the west and to the north and to the south.

Can they all be asleep? Is the child sleeping? Does she grow ever younger in her sleep? Is her dog? Is it her dog? They've only just started hanging out together. Perhaps they met out of a common interest in me. Whatever. She is certainly not walking the halls of River House; all the walking being done tonight is being done by me. But, still... no one reads late into the night? No one sits in front of a flickering TV pondering the loaded gun in a bureau drawer or the sleeping pills in the medicine chest? No one has insomnia, or has forgotten to turn off a lamp, or is on vacation leaving something lit to fool would-be burglars? Apparently not. It's dark out there. Very very dark. If not for the street lamps, Little Sokoki would have only the stars for comfort. And stars are not comforting. Stars dwarf us. Stars put us in our place—a minor solar system in a minor galaxy in a minor key. No wonder so few look up.

Strange, I admit, but even so, this lack of light must happen from time to time, and this is merely one of those times. I guess.

Back to my furniture mountain, which is by now no more than a few more chairs and a chest of some sort. But I can already tell that if there was a door, it's been covered over. I am undaunted. There has to have been a door. What did Akeley do? Climb up and down the fire escape behind the theater to come and go from his house? Wait until dark and turn into a bat? Of course not. There's a door here somewhere and I will find it.

Three of the ballroom walls are outside walls, each with a row of tall windows and each a bearing wall. And one of the ballroom walls is an inside wall. This also seems to be a bearing wall. But behind the small tumble of discarded furniture, I've found a seemingly useless arrangement of curtain walls jutting into the ballroom from the center of the middle outside wall. Aside from cutting off a part of the huge room thereby possibly providing somewhere for catering, these walls seem to have no structural function. Somewhere along one of these curtain walls I will find what I'm looking for.

3 A.M. is not that long from now. Where do I drill first? Studying the curtain walls, tapping for studs, I decide to begin my search where I would put stairs if this were my building and if this overlarge room was once a series of rooms. So where is the most dramatic place possible for an impressive staircase up to my roof house?

Right here. It's in a direct line of sight from the front doors of the ballroom which I am sure stand now as they originally did, even if they are not the original doors.

Using my hand brace and bit, I make two holes in my chosen wall, one for peeking into and another very near to the first hole to insert my laser pointer through. The standard space between either side of a curtain wall of sheetrock is usually three and a half inches. Obviously, my drill will easily go through both pieces of sheetrock.

First try shows me nothing. Doesn't matter. I will keep trying until it does.

Third try (third try is always the lucky one, the magic one)—what's this? The little flexible laser can be either a tiny flashlight or a red pointer beam. Using the pointer beam, I can see that the red dot shining on whatever is on the other side of the wall appears to be some distance away, much further than the far side of the wall would be. What I'm looking for is behind this curtain wall, I'm sure of it.

Good god, suddenly my heart feels sore with fear.

But I will not stop. I have nothing else to do. Nothing. There is nowhere else to go. Nowhere. I thought it would be the river; I thought I would peacefully, easefully, drown. I thought I would simply stop. There would be no capture, no media feed, no trial, no lawyers, no mug shots in the tabloids, no television discussions of why I did it, no gruesome gloating over how I did it, no book written by me in a cell, no waiting, waiting, waiting, until...how does California kill? They give you a choice: lethal injection or gas chamber. I've researched neither. But then I don't have to choose. Now I think something else awaits me. Something that flows directly out of the story I have been living through since the day Kate died, something that started with a small unwatched child wandering away from her home in search of wonder. How do I know she did not find it in a pool of golden fish?

I have to get through this wall. That's what the hand sheetrock saw is for. No fooling around, no thinking twice. I've already done enough damage in this building alone to warrant the worst the law can do. Vermont does not kill, but it does lock up for life—it's not so much the locking up that sets my teeth on edge, though that is bad enough; it's the company—I stab the sheetrock with the saw's triangular point and begin sawing in a curve, working to make an ill-shaped hole large enough for me to crawl through. When that's done, I intend sawing a similar but unavoidably different ill-shaped hole in the back of the curtain wall. And then I can use my large flashlight, the one I bought one day, a million years ago, at Price Chopper, to see what's behind all this.

Bingo. Charles River Akeley's formal staircase. Hardly the worse for wear or for lack of wear.

In nine minutes it will be three o'clock in the morning.

The worst I ever saw him was when he was scheduled to guest on *West Wing*. His role was that of a senior senator from Connecticut who actually terrified Martin Sheen's President Bartlett: a man as educated as Bartlett, as articulate, as sober, as principled, but unlike Bartlett, loved on both sides of the aisle. Reading the script, he told me the part would be a real stretch for him: educated, principled, sober. But it was a good part: strong, complex...and the dialogue snapped with wit, a heady heretical intelligence played out at high speed, not to mention his getting to quote Shakespeare as well as Ralph Waldo Emerson. The moral tale of his true statesman from Connecticut, who suddenly collapses and dies in the Oval Room at the feet of the President of the United States, was supposed to extend over two episodes, but three days before filming he endured what he thought was a massive heart attack and we (his agent and I) rushed him to Cedars-Sinai Hospital.

For hours, enduring test after test, he suffered the torment that comes with terrifying pain and an acute fear of death. He clutched at my hand until my bones cracked. He told me over and over how much he loved me, told me so often I began to wonder who he thought I was. Awash in tears, Kate in my belly unknowingly conceived, I had no idea he was so afraid of dying. I had no idea he was so wracked with the horrors of meeting his maker, or even of just clocking out, of going like my mother and blinking into blackness. I would have thought he'd be relieved to go. It would mean the death of his demon. It would mean his demon would finally shut up.

What I discovered was that his Dad was still in there somewhere, talking up Hell.

In the hospital, he could not drink. He could not fuck. He could not pretend to be somebody else. He was naked and defenseless. He was also not having a heart attack. He was having a panic attack so severe he went into a seizure.

And yet, on the day he was expected, he was ready for the cameras. Doped to his eyeballs on some variety of diazepam or other, he played his part perfectly. But all the time I watched him, I kept remembering a full grown movie star, crawling down a hospital corridor, bare ass in the open air, howling out his eternal human terror.

Thinking about it now, that night was nothing but a prelude to the day our house burnt down. And I was the real heart attack.

Thinking all this, I've had my first moment of doubt. He drank to keep sane, to stop the fear that seeped through his system like some foul gas. And how did he become so frightened? Enter the fanatical father. Did his father kill Kate? But what made his father a fanatic? How far back does it go, all this crazed pain and fear? Where *could* it go back to? How far back is there to go? It goes back to God. In that case, God killed Kate. Fuck God.

These stairs are real. These aren't stairs that come and go, twist and untwist in the back of a person's closet. I have to believe that.

How long since anyone climbed these stairs? There's so little dust. By flashlight, the rich colors of the wood, the fine carpeting, the wallpaper, seem brilliant. Fresh. Clean. Not new. But not old either. There's a smell of furniture wax in here. I'm passing a wall sconce now. Very pretty. Art Nouveau. Not electric. Gas. A second sconce. And a third. I am surprised. You'd think that whoever got rid of the ornate iron scrollwork and the second story porches and railings and pillars would have sold these long ago. And if not, whoever came next (surely Benjamin Willow's father), would have found these lovely lamps and turned over a nice profit on them during his "remodeling" of River House... along with the wood paneling and the hall and stair carpets. And even if Benjamin's father had never looked for, or found, these stairs, then surely whoever built the curtain walls to hide them...? A thought occurs to me, one that couldn't possibly be true. If all this is still here, then perhaps no one has been in the house on the roof for years. And if no one has been there for years, what is still up there?

But no. Impossible. If I owned River House, one of the first things I would have done would be to investigate Charles River Akeley's house. Benjamin Willow inherited it from his father. Even if Benjamin's father had left anything of value in River House, Benjamin himself would not. And yet—everything seems now to be as it was when Akeley himself climbed these stairs.

This is real. This is all real. Even if reality is an illusion, this is a real illusion, one that I could share with others if I knew any others. I want to believe this as I climb the stairs.

At the top there is a fine pair of carved oak doors. The crystal doorknobs, the brass backplates are still here. I am trembling as I reach out to turn the knob on the right hand door, the one with the keyhole. It ought to be locked. *I* would have locked it. Anyone would have left it locked. But it's not locked. Truth is, I never thought it would be. River House doesn't want to lock me out. It wants something else.

I open the doors.

There was a moment, just one, when I horrified myself, when I wanted to stop, to take it back, when the blood was too much, the screaming too much, the surprise and suffering and hurt on his face too much. In that moment, if I could, I would have dragged him from the house by the hand he'd first held out to me.

It was only a moment, but in that moment, I loved him more than I'd ever loved him.

I've always loved him. Before she was my child, he was my child. He doted on me, counted on me... he needed me. When Kate was born, she became the first child, the favored child. But I still held him, still loved him, would have carried him still as I'd always carried him. If only, if only—Kate could also have lived.

For that, I kept going and kept going until not me, but the screaming, stopped.

I stop dead on the threshold. Not only am I looking at the entrance hall to Akeley's little house on the roof, but it's warm, it's softly lit by gaslight, it's furnished as if Lincoln still lived in the White House, and there's the murmur of voices coming from a room to my left. In a movie, this room would be the drawing room. The door is slightly ajar. Feeling suddenly foolish, I switch off my flashlight. Feeling suddenly exposed, vulnerable, even embarrassed—I'm intruding, this is someone's home and that someone is here, with family or friends or both—I think to turn around, to get out and to shut the entrance doors behind me, to go back the way I came. But the way I came was sealed by a curtain wall. How then did these people get here? How do they leave?

Of course. How silly of me. River House has prepared another movie. Mine alone.

From a murmur, the voices in the room grow louder. No, not the voices—one voice. Much louder.

"Hush! I feel a presence."

I'm sure that's what I hear it say. Where

have I heard a sentence like that before? "I feel a presence." Ah, I know. It's the same place that old standby: "Someone is trying to commune with us," or: "Speak to us, oh spirit of the dear departed!" came from. The movies, of course. Sappy crappy dialogue like that comes straight out of Hollywood, vintage films where people are holding séances on dark and stormy nights. Used to be if it wasn't a black & white C feature starring Claude Rains or Bela Lugosi, it was a B feature with Abbott and Costello or Crosby and Hope. These days, the people are moronic teenagers messing about with a Parker Brothers Ouija board; the very same teenagers who are going to spend the next two hours getting themselves slaughtered in full living color in one graphic and gruesome way after the other. I do not laugh. I'm in no mood to laugh. But if the kids of Little Sokoki sneak up to these rooms on the roof of River House to hold séances, I shall throw up.

In this brand new mood, one I haven't felt in a long time: anger, I don't turn around, I don't leave. What I do is walk straight down the thickly carpeted hall and into the room with the door that's slightly ajar.

And once more stop dead. It's not a local gang of trespassing teenagers. I knew it wouldn't be. No Ouija board either. No soon-to-be corpses. But it is a séance in a drawing room just the same. The voice is coming from a bulky woman seated at a large round table, her eyes closed, her large rectangular head thrown back, her hands clasping the hands of the people seated on either side of her. There are nine of them in all. Nine people holding hands. And all nine dressed as if not Lincoln but Calvin Coolidge sat behind a big desk in the White House. Actually, the man to the right of the medium is a dead ringer for Coolidge. Even better, or much worse, another of the men could be Harry fucking Houdini.

Oh, I get it now. I really do get it. I've reached my limit, gone beyond it, way beyond it. Yes God, I've lost my mind. Heart hammering, broken into a sweat, mouth dry, thoughts scattered like dead leaves in the wind. Can't deny it, not anymore. Not only am I insane, but not one of the nine people in front of me, in a room lit by three small guttering candles and dominated by an overweight overwhelming medium in pearls and a turban, notice me, not even when, trembling, I turn my flashlight back on and shine it in each of their faces.

What I feel is, what I feel is, what I do is—I break down. I finally weep. For the first time since he died, I cry. For the first time since he died, I howl out my grief, throw out my arms as if I could catch his hand, as if I could drag him across our kitchen floor, as if we could stagger away from our latest mess, he making clever comments, me laughing at our folly. The flashlight is still in my hand and still shining, streaking across dark wallpaper, dark paintings of dark people in dark frames, dark and heavy furniture, dark curtains, across pale white faces intent on shushing so the medium might feel "the presence."

And no one hears me weep. No one sees me or hears me. It's as if I am the ghost in the room rather than them.

"Imperator, tell us who is here."

As crazy as I obviously am, as unhinged, as

aggrieved, as abandoned by my own once taken-for-granted sanity, I cannot help but wonder which of them she calls Imperator.

And now booms forth the loudest voice of all, and if it's not James Earl Jones as Darth Vader, it might as well be. Coming from the bulging throat of the turbaned medium, it shouts, "We speak now of the One Who Is Lost."

Vader must mean me. It fits. No one better at loss than me. If Vader means me, Vader the Imperator's right, I am lost, though I am not yet dead. But unless one of these people has managed to live well into their eleventh decade, all of those listening are dead, very dead. At least to me. So what could this mean?

If the past haunts the future; can the future haunt the past?

A sudden thump on the table, a sudden breaking of the circle, a sudden scraping back of chair legs on a bare floor. "I've had enough of this," shouts the man who might be Houdini, "This is the bunk!"

"Sit down, Harry," hisses a very dignified man to Harry's right, "and shut up. Mrs. Piper has been kind enough to come all the way from Boston for you, so you just hush."

The man who looks like Houdini, who is certainly called Harry, whose hair is dyed an obvious black and who is shorter than I am, reseats himself—but with a great show of muscular disgust. At which point, the heavy middle-aged woman named Mrs. Piper stands suddenly, not only scraping the legs of her chair but overturning it entirely, stands and points not directly, but close enough, at me. "This one will suffer evil and will do evil. This one has been lost to evil!"

Just in case, I glance behind me. No one there.

Meanwhile, all the long dead eyes in all the long dead heads swing towards me, a me I know they cannot see, a me I know that Mrs. Piper, or something in Mrs. Piper, can see. And I am out of that room before whoever is in Mrs. Piper's head can slice through mine, and I am running down the gaslit hall towards the glass doors that open onto the roof.

Over one long sunny Sunday, lying in our huge bed and laughing, we came up with an idea for a story, something we were sure would play. A romantic comedy (we both loved Thirties romantic comedies), ours had not only romance and comedy, but some actual true grit and a sweet little payoff in a neat twist of irony before the credits rolled. Not for him to play, he admitted that; it called for someone younger, someone more boyish, more quirky, more likable. Someone like John Cusack or Robert Downey Jr. Excited over its prospects and in love, I gave in and agreed to co-write the script with him.

Before Kate, that screenplay was the true beginning of my hatred. At the time though, I wasn't aware it was hatred; I thought it was shame.

He was an actor, and a fine actor, but he wasn't a writer, yet somehow he took over "our" script, and somehow I found myself not the writer, not even the co-writer, but the typist and page layout designer. What I wrote while he was doing something else: acting, sleeping, drinking, he cut. What he wrote, lying on a couch writing longhand on yellow legal tablets, he'd drop off at my desk expecting me to make it look like a screenplay. Once and only once, I managed an entire scene left untouched by him, and when that happened, I found myself lunching in a trendy Santa Monica restaurant with my agent and talking about that scene: reciting it from memory, laughing at my own wit, making sure she knew I was writing, that I was an equal partner, and as I listened to myself babbling on, I knew what I was saying. What I was pleading with her to believe was that the script still had something to do with me, that I hadn't been shunted to the side, reduced to a sort of secretary, yet knowing that in truth I had. My agent is good. She caught the subtext.

Eyes held calm and steady, lips sipping a designer chai, body sculpted and dressed for business, I writhed inside, skittered from morbid thought to morbid thought, utterly humiliated, frantically disgraced by myself.

Somehow he learned about that lunch (not from her, please, not from her, even now I'd like to think I'd earned that much respect), understood the subtext as well as my agent had, and he laughed at me. He laughed. It wasn't funny, that laugh. There was no humor in it. It was round and bullish with contempt. I don't remember what he really said, but I remember what he really meant. He meant that here he was, just an actor, writing rings around me, the well-paid screenwriter and prizewinning novelist. He meant that I knew he'd done it and I had to pretend he hadn't done it. So I had to go out and show off. I had to make sure people thought I was still the best writer in the family.

Actually, he couldn't write rings around me. He couldn't write at all. The finished script, with the exception of my one allowed scene, was, as one writer friend put it, "The Coen Brothers meet a crayon." If he hadn't had such a ravaging need to be brilliant at everything he did, a need so overwhelming it trampled on love, even on simple decency, I could have made it work. I could have made it sing. At the very least, I could have made it make sense. And with my agent's help, I could have sold it to Downey or to Cusack.

But not selling it wasn't the problem. Even his cruelty wasn't the problem. The problem was that I allowed him to do that to me, allowed him to make me feel like that, to kill what I did best.

Why did I do that? I did it for such a simple commonplace reason, one so easy to understand, so easy to see coming no wonder everyone saw it but me. I did it because I believed in him, in his talent, as I did not believe in myself, in my talent. Not then and not now.

And later, why did I allow myself to kill Kate by allowing him to kill Kate? Looking at it now, I see we were in a war. My side wanted to prove itself against such a formidable foe. His side fought against admitting I was a foe at all, but was merely a helpmate and a bedpal. We fought our war until I allowed myself to kill Kate by allowing him to kill her.

In our war, Kate lost.

By cutting him up into little pieces, I have not had the last laugh. There is no last laugh.

In two minutes it will be three in the morning

and I am racing across the high flat roof of River House, away from whatever is going on in Charles River Akeley's roof-house, and towards the tallest tower that sits, as I've already said, like a huge pawn piece at the edge of the roof above the corner of Main Street and High and the actual street corner far below. I look back only once and there are no lights in a single one of Akeley's windows just as there were no lights in Little Sokoki when this long night began, as there are still no lights but streetlamps. Ahead looms the tower and in the tower the south-facing window that must be the way in and the way out.

There is no parapet around the edge of the roof of River House. One could simply take one running step too many and plunge five stories to the concrete below, and for an instant it crosses my mind, it beckons, but—there is a light in the tower.

The window won't open. The double doors at the top of Akeley's staircase opened with ease, but not this window. It's been nailed shut, and over the nail-heads there are who knows how many coats of dark (green, I think) paint slapped on over the years. The window is set at a height that allows me to see that it's hinged, so I know it is meant to open and to close, but too high to look straight into the tower. All I can see is the light coming from something inside shining on the tower ceiling, a domed affair with its four huge dormered windows standing upright as the roof curled over them. I can also see a latch, painted as the window frame and the nails have been painted, over and over until nails, latch, and windowsill are one dark green lumpish thing.

I shall need my hammer. And the new chisel.

There are a number of ways of looking at suicide. Most, if not all, of the world's religions rail against it; believe it to be an act of despair or guilt, like almost everything else their followers might think to do. I think all of this comes from their fear of dying, but even more from their dreadful suspicion that the religion they practice is a load of total hogswollop and no heaven is waiting for them. Nothing is waiting for them but an eternal fade to black.

I'm with the ancient Stoics. The Stoics held "murder of self" in high regard, thought of it as a final act of defiance against the misery of living. Life could and did beat the crap out of the tragic heroine, but suicide allowed her to make that one last nose-thumping gesture of free and glorious will. Of all the illusions, death is the greatest illusion. Suicide shatters it like a hammer shatters a mirror.

At least, I hope so. Especially now.

I remember what Ghandi said, finding hot and cold comfort there: "If I had no sense of humor, I would long ago have committed suicide."

Speaking of humor and hammers, I've splintered the shit out of the old window frame, but it's coming. A few more attempts with the chisel and the painted latch inside is sure to give way.

Once upon a time, suicides were buried at crossroads. I really like that. Those who devised the practice were no doubt protecting themselves from the Evil Eye, but for the suicide it seems to me to be a sort of afterdeath "which way to go now?" I do not grieve, but I certainly do lament I shall not be buried at a crossroad somewhere.

I suddenly wonder: what *will* they do with me?
I have no one but my agent to claim my body, and
lord knows she'll want it disposed of as quickly and
as cheaply as possible. Considering the cost, but
more, the circumstances, I really doubt I'll be laid
to fuss and thrash about (no rest for the wicked)
next to Kate or to him. And I know she won't
bother looking for my mother who's in a small box
in a concrete wall of small boxes somewhere in
Marin County, California. I imagine she'll cremate
me, fling the ashes into the nearest trashcan. No,
hold on. She's a gardener. She'll use me for mulch
or whatever—fuck it. None of the others are where
their bodies were left to rot, and I won't be here, or
there, either.

As for the dying itself, there are so many ways
to go, it can get downright confusing. Even before
the crossroads, us suicides have so much to choose
from. James Leo Herlihy, the writer of *Midnight
Cowboy*, chose sleeping pills. George Sanders,
lonely, bewildered, and alone in Barcelona of all
places, also took pills. But George's last note had
style; in it he claimed he'd died of boredom. Hart
Crane jumped off a cruise ship, which assumes
that at some point he felt good enough to be
taking a cruise, calling out as he leapt, "Goodbye,
everybody!" Sounds quite jolly. The very unjolly
Yukio Mishima made his suicide a political
statement by disemboweling himself. Just behind
him, as tradition dictates, stood a fellow traveler
ready to deliver the killing blow to the back of his
neck. It took three killing blows, and two fellow
travelers. Triple ouch. With his youngest daughter
only six months old, poet John Berryman jumped

to his death off the Washington Avenue Bridge
in Minneapolis, but not until after waving to
passerbys: "Yoohoooo! Hello there! Byeee!" Maybe
Jim Morrison, possible poet, broke on through to
the other side in his Paris bathtub with a drug
overdose, and maybe he didn't. He probably did:
drunk, stupid, and vain as he was, because if he's
still alive, he'd be the first to tell us. Charlotte
Mew, who might have gained a larger place in the
Hall of Poetic Fame had she bothered to live, drank
disinfectant. Diane Arbus made doubly sure; for
her it was pills and a razor blade. Two months
after publishing to great acclaim the thereafter
badly neglected novel *Raintree County*, Ross
Lockridge Jr. gassed himself in his garage. That
seems popular.

Has an artist ever jumped off a roof?

He was told by a reliable source (an actual
cop in the actual New York City police force) that
the most efficient way to commit suicide was to
use a .38 caliber revolver. But because folks in
extremis so often missed when using a handgun, or
turned themselves into instant root vegetables, the
revolver had to be loaded with hollow point bullets.
The cop explained that hollow points disintegrate
on impact—no chance of surviving when that
happened. (Although Don Carpenter managed
his small handgun well enough for the job. A
good friend of fellow suicide Richard Brautigan,
Carpenter was a writer who wrote about Hollywood
like it was really Hollywood: hard and cruel and
painful and almost always a dead-end.)

We both found the inside tip quite interesting,
but, said he, if he ever decided to kill himself, he

wouldn't use a gun, no matter how efficient. He said he'd drink himself to death. I said that, like Dylan Thomas and Nick Nolte, he was already doing that. He said fuck you. So I said if I were to kill myself, being a woman, I couldn't possibly use a gun—I mean, as Brautigan's last written words had pointed out, guns were pretty messy. I thought drowning sounded about right. No pain. No blood. No mutilation. No getting found with your neck stretched to some disgusting length and your face a tornado blue. No getting your head pulled out of a toilet. But drowning in deep water, well...your hair does such lovely things down there, that is, for the first few days or so. Think of Shelley Winters drifting about with pond weed in *A Place in the Sun*. He laughed. I laughed. It was a golden afternoon by the green and golden sea and neither one of us believed we'd ever kill ourselves. After all, he was a successful movie star, I was a successful writer, and Kate was a successful toddler. All three of us lived in Malibu. Who kills themselves in Malibu?

I'm sitting on the cold roof, my back against the tower, drinking straight from the bottle. Window's open. I pried it open with my old hammer and my new chisel. I'm pretty sure I've made another of my messes and this time there's no ceiling tiles to cover it up. It doesn't matter. By the time someone notices, and that someone is bound to be the maintenance man who shops where I shop, a few years could have come and gone. By then, I won't give a shit. Me, I'm working up the nerve to climb through the window. The light inside the tallest tower has grown brighter and there's music just as there was music before, only this music isn't Cole

Porter. It's nothing like Cole Porter. This is more
like a turn-of-the-century hurdy-gurdy: organ and
trumpet. It's strangely familiar but not familiar
enough for me to name it. No one's singing; there
are no lyrics. Shivering, I lean back listening, and
slugging down the red wine. Still no sound from
the streets below. I haven't heard a single car,
a single voice, a single dog or cat or cow (this is,
after all, Vermont), a single noise aside from my
own noise, and now this music, since I locked my
apartment down on the third floor ages and ages
ago. Days ago, months ago, a minute ago. Who
knows anymore? I think time has stopped being
a dimension, at least for me. I think it's standing
still. I think it's a permanent three in the morning.
Something else I think is that I no longer exist in
the same place everyone else exists in...not since
I invited the young man into my room. Or maybe
not since I made that other mess in the faraway
kitchen. (Closet, wall in my room, bathtub, door to
the ballroom, curtain wall in the ballroom, window
in the corner tower: if I owned this building, I'd
evict me on the spot.) I think something happened
somewhere along the way that changed everything.
That's what I think. But who cares what I think?
It's how I'm feeling that's beginning to worry
me. Am I frightened? Oh yes, oh my god, I am
frightened. Scared enough to swallow my tongue.

What's this? There's no more wine in my bottle.
I drank the whole thing? In what, two minutes?
Holy shit. Now what? Leave it on the roof? Or
throw it as far as I can, listening for the sound of
its sudden smash on the street below? I'd never
do that. What if I hit someone? Even if I missed,
still, what about the glass all over the street, glass

shards scattered all over the sidewalk? Tomorrow, when I am no longer here, a little kid could cut her little feet. Or a dog, his innocent doggy pads. Or a heifer, her new-born hooves. In Little Sokoki, heifers often wander the streets. It's that kind of town.

I stand up and throw the bottle as far as I can, practically dislocate my shoulder doing it, and yes, there is a distant smash of glass on the ground far below.

Last chance. Will someone now open their window in outrage? Will they see me, yell at me, call the cops on me? Will they save my strange and useless life? I must want them to. I threw the bottle, didn't I?

Nothing. Nothing happens. No lights go on. No windows open. No furious curious head sticks out. Nothing. Nothing. Nothing. I am alone in this illusion. It's all mine.

There's nothing left to do but climb in the window.

I climb in the window, which isn't easy with a tool-belt full of tools to drag through with me.

I knew she'd be there. I knew she'd be Kate's age by the time I got into the tower. If it was ever psoriasis on her face and her neck, it isn't psoriasis now. It's pond weed, bright green duck weed, the kind that floats on the top of the water. I didn't know she'd have the dog. But he's there too, smiling at me. She isn't, but he is...a big sloppy bloody doggy smile. She's staring at me. Nothing more. Nothing less. Staring at me. Like bad snapshots, the center of her eyes are red. I've been humiliated since I came here by the visions of other artists, better artists—is this my final, my worst, punishment? To have the ugly woman turn into a sly girl turn into a threatening child turn into a terrifying toddler turn into my Kate? And the dog? He's a small dog now, small and black with dots of tan over his eyes, on the tip of his tail. Am I supposed to believe it's my dog, my Prince, the one I caused to be run over by a car because I was a child and he was a puppy and we neither of us knew that life could kill?

They're both standing as far from the entrance window as they can get. There really isn't much room anywhere else since the whole of the tower is taken up by something enormous hanging from the high central ceiling boss.

This isn't what Faye found waiting for her at the top of the stairs in *The Windigo's Daughter*. Somehow it's worse. Faye found her true shape, her true self. What have I found?

Faye means to run in her house and to shut her door and never come out again. But in her fear—and because of the skirt over her head—she runs ever and ever closer to the sugar saplings at the edge of her lawn, saplings like doorjambs. Wherever she goes, she is followed by the swarm of buzzing bees. More and more of them clinging to her arms, to her legs, to the red dress. Faye, once red, is now black and yellow with bees.

The bees drive Faye to the very threshold of the sapling door. But she digs in her heels and she does not tremble, not Faye—for Faye is not only as willful as a willow root, she is

*as brave as a bramble. And she will not go
back through the door, no, she won't. All the
bees in the world, all the bees in any other
world, could not make her. Go ahead and try,
she says, go ahead and try. They could sting
her to death if they liked, and she would not
budge. Why should she go back? It was her
door. She had made it to enter this world and
when she felt like it, and only then, she'd use
it to go home. But not before.*

*But the biggest bee, the bee that has been
Mr. Honig, does a truly ghastly thing. He does
something that cows even Faye. He calls
on the name of Manitou. Faye slaps at Mr.
Honig—but misses. She would rend him limb
from limb if he were still a traveling man. She
would swallow him whole. Faye is furious in
her fear. She backs up a step, taking all the
bees with her. But she knows she's doomed,
knows it at the name of Manitou, for now she
feels something old and cold and timeless and
bold touch her soul. And she senses what it
is immediately. It is her own true body, her
own true form, checked on the other side of the
door like a cloak in a cloakroom, returned to
her.*

*Faye opens her mouth, a huge mouth
suddenly sprung with an orange gumful of
crooked yellow teeth, big teeth, long teeth,
pointed. She howls. A howl that fills up
West Hackmatack Street with the Windigo's
daughter she was, the Windigo's daughter she
is once again, the Windigo's daughter she will
ever be.*

What's waiting for me in the tower, aside
from the small child, the dog, and the hurdy-
gurdy music, is a large box. No, not a box. It's
too handsome to be called merely a box. It's a
cabinet made of mahogany or walnut or some dark
expensive wood, and inside it's lined with polished
metal. I can tell it's lined with some sort of metal
because one of the sides of the box is plate glass.
Not only is it a cabinet, it's a tank. It's a tank full
of water, and it's suspended from the ceiling by a
thick strong chain. Tears running down my face,
I foolishly look for the fish. Goldfish, piranha,
barracuda, whatever. Of course there are no
fish. Over the tank, and between it and the ceiling
attachments, hangs a kind of wooden arrangement
which seems more like colonial stocks than a lid.
It has two holes in it. So soon as I see the holes, I
know it is not a lid; it really is a stocks. And I know
what the holes are for. So does the child. For the
first time I hear her speak. In a lilting childish lisp,
she says, "It's his 'upside down.' Up there is where
he puts his feet. He hangs by his feet. You're
supposed to hang by your feet."

Why would I put my feet in the holes? Why
would I hang by my feet in a tank of water? Who
puts his feet in an "upside down"? But something
about her voice hurts. It's not Kate. It's not Kate's
voice. The dog is not Prince. It's not my Prince who
died racing along behind the wheels of my bike.
But it still hurts. It hurts every bit as much as if
they were.

Not getting any closer to the child or the dog
than I can manage, I work myself around the
hanging cabinet. On one side there's a brassbound
wooden ladder that leads up to the wooden stocks

with the holes in it. Hanging above the stocks is the actual lid, a heavy wooden cover with chains dangling from it. And a huge padlock attached to a large link in the longest chain. The ladder explains how one gets up and into the tank and the padlock explains the insanity of doing it at all (he hangs from his feet upside down in a tank of water and allows himself to be padlocked in: oh god, of all the ways I've thought of killing myself, this one never once occurred to me, although I'll give it this: it *is* a way to drown)...but I still can't tell where the light in the tower is coming from. I can't see a lighting fixture anywhere, but the light is a hard white light and makes everything too clear, too sharp, too real.

Too horrid.

If this is what I have chosen for myself, if this is how it ends, then not only am I insane, I am cruel. But am I, after all, Houdini?

By now, I can't see either the dog or the child. They're both on the other side of the tank. But I can hear them. The dog is licking his chops, then panting, then licking his chops some more, and the child is still talking. She's saying, "If you get in it like you're s'posed to, you'll drown. 'Less you can get out. He can get out. Bet you can't."

And all this time, the music plays on and on and I don't know what it is, but she does. I don't ask; I haven't said a thing. She tells me the name of the song. "It's called *Asleep in the Deep.* He plays it when he's in his 'upside down'."

With the name of the song said aloud, someone long ago and far away begins to sing. *Loudly the bell in the old tower rings/Bidding us list to the warning it brings:/Sailor, take care! Sailor, take care!/Danger is near thee, beware!/Beware!*

*Beware! Beware!/Many brave hearts are asleep in
the deep,/So beware! Beware!*

I don't ask who "he" is. I know who he is. He's
at a séance in the candle-lit drawing room in the
roof house of Charles River Akeley, and for him it's
somewhere in the Nineteen Twenties. He has only
a few years to live, but apparently he has forever to
be dead.

I may be insane. I may be suicidal. I'm really
sorry to say that I am certainly homicidal—although
killing wasn't something I aspired to growing up. I
grew up wanting to be safe, to be admired, to be
loved. We all want that, though few of us kill to get
it. But River House is haunted. As I said, I may be
insane, but I'm not a fool. It's in the Forties, and
Louise Brooks is in my room drinking and reading
and deciding to write because writers don't kill
themselves. It's sometime in the Twenties: Harry
Houdini is up in the roof house attending a séance
that eternally cheeses him off, while HP Lovecraft
stands at a lower window imagining another of
his ghastly stories. On the second floor, Alfred
Hitchcock is making movies in the late Fifties.
Maybe Cole Porter's here and maybe he isn't. But
someone is, and that someone is playing his music.
Shirley Jackson sees River House as Hill House.
It's the early Sixties and she's hallucinating in her
room which must be my room since she's climbing
my stairs. The stairs are really here; they exist in
one version or another in one version or another
of River House. Shirley found hers. I found mine.
Because of the stairs, Shirley wrote *The Haunting
of Hill House*. I'm not Shirley Jackson who never
wrote a bad sentence. I'm not Louise Brooks who,
whether she gave a shit or not, became an icon

of early Hollywood. I'm not Alfred Hitchcock who made movies that will be seen by people a hundred years from now. I'm not Lovecraft who wasn't that great a writer, but who was a first rate fabulist.

But I might just be Houdini.

I can see out the tall bowed-top window, the one I'm standing nearest. Of the four, it's the east facing window, the one that looks directly out over the Connecticut River. I can't see much of anything, it's so dark, so quiet, the light is so bright in the tower, the glass in the one hundred and forty-four year old window too warped and wavy. Whoever or whatever I saw the day I went swimming in the river had to have stood right here. Stood right here and looked down at me wet and dripping on the island. Was the cabinet hanging here then? Was the music playing?

Right about now, the mood I'm in, which is a mix of helpless terror, advancing madness, and abject resignation, I imagine it was someone taking a break from the ongoing séance over in Akeley's place.

The child is still speaking. Over and over, she says, "Get in the tank. Get in the tank. Get in the tank." It's become a little Shirley Temple song, not an order, but a jingle.

It's hopeless. I begin to climb what I think is my last ladder.

I not only took his heart, I took his head. But though I kept his heart—after all, he said it was mine, he gave it to me—I did not keep his head. I left his head where it belonged, in the pond where

she died. It's there now, feeding the goldfish, and
there it will stay. Someone someday will find it,
but not for a long long time. When Kate died, our
neighbors said they would drain the pond, dig it
up, destroy it. But we both said no, no, please...it's
Kate's pond. Please don't punish the pond. It's the
last place she ever saw. And how do we know if she
knew Glory there? How do we know if as she died
she spoke to the fish and they to her? We know so
little of life and of death, how do we know what her
dying was like?

We begged them to keep the pond. We said it's
a beautiful pond. An old pond. There's a mermaid
of blue stone there, her tail trailing in the water.
There are water lilies that spread out petals like
clotted white cream, their centers the delicate pink
of Kate's skin. There's pond weed through which
from time to time one can see the golden fish flash
by.

On the surface, like green lace, there's duck
weed.

They kept the pond. They will keep the pond.
The house has been theirs for years, and it shall
no doubt be theirs for many more years. They are
old Malibu money, there before the rich and their
"colony" shouldered out the beach. They will not
sell the house.

His head will stay where it is. Maybe not yet,
but in time it will be a palace for fish who will swim
in and out of his eyes, flicking their golden tails.

At the top of the ladder, there's a small
platform. Somehow I know it's here Houdini
would stand and allow himself to be handcuffed,
straight-jacketed, and have his bare feet placed

through the mahogany stocks, which were then clamped and locked into position. So soon as that was done, the stocks would carefully be drawn up, taking an upside down, trussed up and manacled Houdini along with it, until he dangled headfirst and seemingly helpless over the open tank. Then it would be slowly slowly lowered and lowered until almost his entire body would be submerged, his head almost touching the bottom of the water-filled tank. To make it all that much worse, that much more dramatic, a wooden lid would be lowered onto the top of the tank, and padlocked shut. At this point someone would draw a curtain around the cabinet. The audience could no longer see Houdini, but they could hear him struggling to release himself. It took two whole breathless minutes, but in time, every time, he'd appear from around the back of the water-filled cabinet, dripping wet, exhausted, freed of each of his bonds, and triumphant.

Gazing down into the tank, I think: what a crazy thing to do. I think I understand drowning. But not like this. Something could have gone wrong at any time. How could he stand the stress of doing what he did, performance after performance? And why?

Dotty Parker wrote: *Razors pain you; Rivers are damp; Acids stain you; And drugs cause cramp. Guns aren't lawful; Nooses give; Gas smells awful; You might as well live.* What the clever self-hating little Jewish girl from Jersey neglected to mention is that all these small annoyances are as brief as a passing hail storm. But not this. Two minutes upside down and drowning. Not if I can help it.

After he called me Houdini Heart, I looked

Harry up on the internet. E. L. Doctorow put it like this: "He was so insanely devoted to what he was doing and so disciplined that the ultimate insanity of his life never occurred to him."

I stand at the top of his ladder and I agree with Doctorow with all that remains of my heart. This is completely nuts. Never mind what he was doing. What am I doing?

Whatever I think I'm doing, Harry needed help for all this. I have no help. Or maybe the little girl means to help me. But unless she's taken her Alice in Wonderland pill and is now growing larger and larger, she can't.

What now?

Philip Massinger, the second-rate Seventeenth Century playwright, but first-rate portrayer of women, wrote: "If you like not hanging, drown yourself; Take some course for your reputation."

For my reputation, such as it is, would I both hang and drown myself?

I sit down on the platform, take off my tool-belt, my hat, my sweater, my shoes, my socks. Dropping them off the platform, the tool-belt and its contents make a terrific racket when they hit the floor far below. Wearing only a black tee tucked into tight black pants, I place my naked feet in the half stocks, close the other half over it, and am now effectively locked into place. I could still open the thing, still get out—but the little girl is chanting and the dog is panting and Houdini's *Asleep in the Deep* is playing over and over.

At this point someone should be locking the stocks, and someone else should begin pulling me up somehow, perhaps by hauling hand-over-

hand on one particular set of chains. Looking
at it, I see the thing is a simple block and tackle
device. It's basically an engine hoist, a looped
chain. Depending on which side you pull, it'll raise
or lower an engine block at virtually the touch of
a finger. I can hoist myself up, lower myself down
with great ease. So who will lock my stocks and
who will pull on my chains? Me, that's who. After
all, there's no one up here but me...with the key,
which I will hide under my tongue. No strait jacket,
no locked lid, perhaps not even a demure curtain
pulled across the plate glass so no one can see
my struggles. So that no one can see I have a key
under my tongue. As for cheating with the key: this
is my first and probably last time. I'm due a break
here.

I understand now. This is my test. It's rather
like tying a woman into a ducking stool. If she lives
through the long and breathless immersion, she's a
witch; if she drowns, she's innocent.

But who tests me. The dog? The child? Who
tests me, if not me myself? If I have done all this,
then I was right in the first place. Reality is an
illusion and this illusion is mine and mine alone.
If I have not done all this, then I am wrong and I
understand nothing about reality, nothing—just
like everyone else. No matter if they call themselves
Pope or Ayatollah or Guru, or if they speak out as
a worthy and respected scientist, or as a brilliant
philosopher, not one of us really knows a true
thing about reality. Socrates said that to know one
knows nothing is the mark of an intelligent man. I
know nothing. I wish that meant I had talent. I
wish that meant I could write. I wish that meant
I could change the past. I wish, I wish, I wish...if

wishes were fishes, even the guilty could swim.

If I am wrong and River House is alive in some way, as alive and as malevolent as Shirley's Hill House was meant to be, or, heaven forbid, as King's Overlook Hotel, then I am trapped here. No choices for me: River House has made all the running. I cannot flee. I cannot stay locked in my room. I cannot seek help. I can't even give myself up to the Law. I can do nothing but what River House intends me to do. Is this because I belong here? Or because I don't belong here?

No end to my questions. No end to my suffering. Unless death is an end. Is it? I don't know.

Houdini never understood a thing about illusion; he thought the word "illusion" meant "trick." From his point of view, he played cunning tricks on his audience, while mediums tried to play shabby tricks on him. A trickster outraged at the tricks of others, Houdini spent his life working to debunk them.

I know the answer to my question now. Am I Houdini? No, I am not Houdini. I am much better than a trickster—or much worse. I believe illusion is what reality is made of. I do not fool around. What I do, I do for real, and trust that my own hidden (at least to me) intentions will form the reality I seek. I also trust—I have to, no way to know for sure—that the reality I see around me is the reality I sought.

I do know this. I set out to die for my sins, for I am a true-blue genuine first class sinner, and I will die.

The irony here is that not only will I drown, and

in a tower of all places, but that in dying I will still prove not a Catholic but a witch.

I begin pulling on the chains. It works. The stocks slowly rises bringing with it my firmly padlocked feet. To keep from rubbing the skin from his ankles, Houdini has had the holes lined with sheepskin. I thank him for this. I've always expected to be frightened, but never intended to experience pain. I'm not good at pain. If there was pain, I would be almost certain to stop. And I can stop. But as I've said before, self-chosen or compelled, I have nothing else to do. Though I really can't see how I shall manage to lift myself high enough to dangle over the tank, or to lower myself into it. I've always had strong legs, but weak arms. Yet I keep going. If I am meant to do this, it will be done. I can't believe I am meant merely to try to do this and to fail. If so, nothing would make sense, nothing. And in the last few moments, much that has seemed senseless becomes meaningful. Perhaps not to a rational mind, but to one now purely instinctual, purely magical, partly mad, partly sad, and purely suicidal, it makes the utmost sense.

Sometime in his teens, he became convinced he would die young. He believed all great artists die young. Unwavering in this conviction, he also thought the last gasp of youth meant somewhere around the mid Thirties. To prove this, he recited a goodly list of those who had gone before him: Bobby Darin, Buddy Holly, River Phoenix, James Dean, Jean Harlow, Jimi Hendrix, John Belushi, Carole Lombard, Marilyn Monroe. I stopped him at Doc Holliday. With the possible exception of Holliday, I said, not one of those you've named was a great artist. These, said I, are the great artists who died young: John Keats, Wilfred Owen, Rupert Brooke, Nick Drake, Dylan Thomas, Marlowe and Shelley and Mozart and Byron, not forgetting all the Brontes, even Branwell Bronte, who admittedly was no artist at all, but still managed a short life by depression or debauchery, I forget which.

I made him laugh. But not for long.

The night before his thirty-sixth birthday, he began to panic. He was still alive. He was just about to pass into the last of his Thirties. This could only mean one of two things: either he was just about to die, or he was not a great artist. Either interpretation made him ill with fear.

We both sat up all that night, him freaking and drinking and sniveling and writing rather funny farewell notes to mostly me, but some to the world. I sat up holding him, stroking him, trying to calm him. But he was well and truly convinced he would die, if not that night, then on the morrow. How, he had no idea. But that he would, he harbored not a shadow of a doubt.

I'm still amazed he remained coherent considering the amount of booze he put away, not to mention the Valium he swallowed.

He lived.

I shall always believe he was gravely disappointed to survive that night and the following day. I shall always believe his not dying on or about his thirty-sixth birthday was the beginning of his doubt about his talent, a doubt that only grew as the years passed. Being as talented after his birthday as he was before his birthday made not a jot of difference to him. He was sure that at any moment someone would find him out, and he would begin the long road down to obscurity.

Believing as I do in the power of belief, I did not laugh.

Until all that has happened, happened, I held no beliefs about my own death. Like most people I thought of my personal demise as seldom as possible, and when I did, the thoughts were idle, slightly silly. Like most people I hoped death would come swiftly, painlessly, and without preamble. In other words: whap! you're gone.

Since Kate died, I've thought of nothing but death.

I pull on the chains and I rise. I pull and I rise still farther. It's easier than I thought it would be. It's more painful as well. Not only my ankles, but my back and my neck hurt. Lack of exercise. What else could it be? After all, I haven't seen the inside of a gym for I don't know how long. I'm thin but not toned. I haven't run other than the chase through the halls of River House...whenever that was. (So odd to think I raced after a child, meaning to hurt her. But then, at the time she wasn't a child; she was still an older woman. Or a young woman. As already said, I begin to forget my time in River House. I also begin to mix up my memories. What came before what? What caused this or caused that? How much that I recall were dreams? Did I dream at all? How long have I been here?) It's hardly surprising my body might complain at being hung upside down. Though how I am to maneuver myself over the watery tank is still a problem. I shall face that when I get there, literally.

I'm off the platform now, my head inches from the wood, the blood rushing into my brain. The music has not stopped, if anything it's become louder, drowning out the chanting child and the panting dog. I am grateful for this small mercy. A few more pulls and I will hang far enough above the surface of the tank water to begin to lower myself down. And that has to be done quickly. If not, I waste precious time getting to the bottom, and in Houdini's Chinese Water Torture, even for someone not padlocked into a strait jacket, there is no time to waste. It will take all the strength I have left to pull myself back up the chains and out of the water before I drown. Do I right myself? Do I go back up as I went down, head down, feet up?

This is where I really need a pair of helping hands. Just a small push would get me where I need to be. There are no hands but mine, and I'm using them on the chains. There's the child, of course, but she's grown much too young to climb the ladder. The dog would be useless even if he got up here, which I hope he does not.

I begin to wriggle, trying to make myself sway a bit, and then possibly to swing. The idea is to force the hinged rod above the tank to move by my movements.

And it does. Inch by inch, and then a jump of half a foot, then a few more inches, and I swing out over the water. Being upside down, I can't easily see the tank. What I see are my hands gripping the chains and my feet in padlocked stocks fastened to the high domed ceiling above me. I should also be able to see out all four of the windows. But with the tower lit as it's lit, all four windows are like mirrors, dark mirrors reflecting back only me—and the tank. And behind the tank, a small and serious child with straight black hair, her hand on the quiet head of a small black dog. They stand waiting, both of them, looking up at me. Momentarily, I think that surely anyone looking at what is after all a landmark that can be seen for miles must have seen me by now? But then I know they can't. For all save the child and the dog, I am a ghost. When did I become a ghost? The tower I hang in is not the same tower that looks over Little Sokoki. For all I know, it is broad daylight and a parade trombones its way up Main Street. For all I know, it's the Twenty-Second Century and River House was torn down years ago. For all I know, Harry Houdini is right this minute attending a séance in the once home of Charles River Akeley and less than an hour ago I was the star attraction.

For all I know, these and a million other moments are taking place all around me, and they always will be, but I have chosen only this one moment to remain in, perhaps forever. My own perfect, perfectly strange, and perfectly awful moment. My own River House. My own hell.

It's now I must lower myself quickly into the water, and now that I am supposed to slip the key to the padlocked stocks under my tongue. I loosen my grip on the chains, begin my slide, headfirst towards the tank, and at the first touch of water on the top of my head, I take in air, enough air to keep me alive...for how long?

For as long as it takes.

And then it occurs to me. Fucking hell. I have no key. There never was a key. I must have been dreaming I had a key.

This is bullshit. If this is what River House wants, it can go screw itself. Even if what I see and what I hear and what I do is an even bigger illusion than life itself, I'm not doing this. I'm not Polanski's tenant driven again and again to jump from his window by whatever corruption occupies the room he's rented. I am a writer. Not a great writer, but not so bloody bad I end like this. Or a story of mine ends like this.

There must be a better ending. There always is. You just have to take your time, never rush, even if every producer in Hollywood is talking about needing the script yesterday.

It takes no time at all to pull myself back to the platform at the top of the tank. No time to release the unlocked stocks, to climb back down the ladder. I quickly dress, quickly refill and rehook my belt so I can crawl out the hinged window and back onto the roof of River House. And where was she all this time? Or her dog? Gone.

Where did they go? Honestly? By now? Who the fuck cares?

If she's me, young again...so? If she's Kate showing me a life she wasn't allowed to live... too late. I can't help her. If she's even my damn mother who's finally allowed me inside River House, well fuck her too. I'll crouch here in the dark until I make up my mind what to do.

Not River House. Me. I'll decide.

The hunger's come back. This time I can't ignore it. If this isn't the time to do as I've always intended, when is?

You might think it too old by now, but it's not. I never needed it to last that long, just long enough for the moment I knew all along was coming. Which is why I pickled it in an ill-smelling ill-used room in a Motel 6 on the edge of Sacramento, California. In its sealed jar, his heart could last for years.

Unlike myself.

Soaked in cloves and allspice and bay and garlic, it's rather nice.

I was always a good cook.

From where I sit, which is where I sat before I broke into the tower, I have to turn to see there's no light in the tower windows. It's as dark as it's been every night since I moved in, every night that is, but this night. All light's off now. Window's closed. I don't remember closing it, but I suppose I did. As for the little house on the roof, Charles River Akeley's house, I need only to look ahead to see that all the windows facing me are lit. Before, at the séance, it was gaslit. I think. But now, in each window there shines one candle. From where I once again sit, cold back against the cold tower wall, cold butt on the sleek black flat roof of River House, Akeley's secret house looks warm. It looks charming. It touches the sentimental sap in me, the part that oooohs and aaaaahs over winter scenes on Christmas cards. It's the house I would have had if I'd ever had the house I truly loved. There's nothing like it in Los Angeles. Houses like this only exist in novels and movies. Of course, if it were mine, it would be on the ground somewhere, surrounded by a gate and a garden, not on the roof of a once hotel.

Slowly chewing, I can't take my eyes off it.

What will River House conjure up now?

239

Time to find out. I close the empty jar and slip it back into my belt. No making messes, not me (but I did throw an empty bottle down into Main Street, didn't I?), and no leaving evidence. There's the camcorder. Should I use the boy's camcorder and finish his film for him? No. I have all the film I need stored right in my head. Too much film. I open the camcorder and yank out his evidence or work or whatever he thought it. Ruined now, I tie it in a huge bow on the latch of the tower window. And then I notice the illuminated church spire clock a block or so up Main Street. Four fourteen in the morning. I'm not surprised. I am beyond surprise, though I am not beyond fear. Or curiosity.

Time to pad across the smooth black roof of River House—what did Benjamin Willow cover it with, rubber?—and find out what awaits me. The tower was nothing, a bit of showmanship, a scene thrown in for its scare value. The little house is the real thing. It makes no sense. It shouldn't be there. Anyone come back from the Gold Mines of Old Califorlorn to build a hotel big enough and grand enough to rub his success in the eye of Little Sokoki, would also have built himself a mansion on one of the hills overlooking the town. From there he could look down, while everyone else had to look up. He would have erected one of those houses found all over America, a grand, overdone, tasteless, somehow hilarious, and thoroughly wonderful robber baron's house. By now it would be called the old Akeley place and Little Sokoki would be as proud of it as it had once hated its builder.

So. No. Though I found it on the blueprints on the wall of Benjamin Willow's office, it was never really Benjamin's office, not the second time I came calling, so this little house exists only for me. Which means, it's mine.

After the right time to eat, it's the right time to take possession.

I pad across the roof and open the door.

There comes a rumbling and a roaring and a cracking of solid rock—craaaakkk! Dirt clods, bits of root, shattered shells from ancient seas, old pot shards, fragments of podzol and brimstone, of jet and chert and tufa and wacke, erupt like Old Faithful from Faye's back lawn, spraying her little brown house with muck. Where a second before there was a table under a tent, now there's a deep black fissure, spitting up slurps and lallops of heart's mud, blowing huge sticky bubbles of urk.

Manitou pokes out a nose. Furiously sniffs the ruined air. The great snout lifts skywards, the nostrils red, each nostril as large as a whale's blowhole. Up comes the rest of the tremendous head, eyeballs rolling.

The Windigo's daughter, stinking as a windigo stinks, dark red hair matted from bulging forehead to high-arched bigfoot, sinks into her hairy skin, grunts in fear as Manitou pulls back its lips to say: GO HOME, ALL OF YOU!

Everyone is here. All of them. Each in their own way has scared me, tormented me, disturbed me. This time, they terrify me. I search their faces. Is he there? Is the boy I left in the shower among them? Is Kate?

No. But then, they wouldn't be, would they? I did not create them, I destroyed them. This is not about what I have unmade, but what I have made. Anarchy and destruction have no home here.

They're not staring at me. Not one of them, not even the child or the dog or Harry Houdini is paying me the slightest mind. They're all staring at the roof ten feet to my right. And then—they aren't. They're turning as one. They're moving. They're running straight at me and as they run they're melting. Melting? Is that the right word? No. The right word is transforming. They're becoming something else. Like bees. And not like bees.

I see. I'm not going to spend a year of my life in a trial as public and as culturally revealing as the trial of the revolting O.J. Simpson. I am not going to lie in a cold room strapped to a cold table to be injected with something humanely lethal. I am not going to drown in the tea-colored Connecticut River. I'm not even going insane, although I may be what folks on this side of the door call dead. Aside from that, what I am doing is being herded by talking bees into my own dream, my own world, somewhere I created.

It's where I belong. It's what I deserve. It is my center and it holds...nothing but me.

Inside the house is outside the house. Inside is a wild and wonderful land, full of wild and wonderful people—but more wonderful still, are its creatures.

242

It isn't yet called Vermont, but it will be.

At that time, magic walked the earth by day and by night, and the very air shivered with an ancient pizzazz.

Stinking, shaggy with matted red fur, I slouch with slow thighs through a sapling door into *The Windigo's Daughter.*

I *am* the Windigo's Daughter.

He was right. I have a Houdini Heart.

Manitou's breath is like a great wind sweeping down from the top of the world. Turning the bees into the leaves of autumn, blowing them back through the sapling door. From the moment they gain the other side, leaves of red and gold, leaves of tender yellow, spring up from the earth as they truly are, as Manogemassak, as the little people, faces like ax blades, hearts like water, giggling as they scatter on home. The Windigo's daughter has at least the grim satisfaction of seeing that the bee, the leaf, the man she married, is no less than a minor Prince of the Manogemassak.

YOU! roars Manitou. WINDIGO'S DAUGHTER! RUN HOME WHILE YOU CAN. RUN HOME TO YOUR FATHER'S HOUSE.

As the Windigo's youngest daughter tumbles through the sapling door, as her father's waiting hairy hand reaches out to snatch her up, comes the last words of Manitou: AND SHUT THE DOOR! I KEEP NO OPEN HOUSE!

Thrice her size, a hundred times her age, the old Windigo stuffs his errant daughter under his reeking armpit, lolloping off through the woods on the other side of the sapling door.

Which exists no more, not now that Manitou has blown them away before sinking back into the earth under West Hackmatack Street.

8318557R0

Made in the USA
Charleston, SC
27 May 2011